I0536643

RIPPED

Olivia Rigal

This book is a work of fiction.
Even if some locations depicted do exist,
the story and event described are totally fictitious
The names, the characters, and the events described have been imagined
by the author. Any resemblance with reality would be a coincidence.

Lady O / Lady O Publishing
www.ladyopublishing.com

Ripped— 1st ed.
ISBN 978-0-9898550-7-5

Special thanks to:

Okay Creation
for the cover design

Contents

FIRST PART
- 1978-

Chapter 1

Manhattan is so pretty around the holidays, I'm happy Ten was able to whisk me away. I still can't believe my mother said yes and let me go with him. But then again, it's hard to say no to a Clark, especially to Tennessee Charles Clark when he puts on his charm. Ten and I have known each other forever, since my parents moved to Long Island and opened their diner. I was so young then, it seems like forever.

In the summer the entire Clark family sets up residence in the Hamptons. It's a tradition and the Clarks are all about traditions. One of those is that the entire clan goes out for brunch on Sundays and wherever they go becomes the trendy place. My parents were lucky; James Tennessee Clark, the patriarch, stopped at their diner and liked it enough to create a new tradition. James Clark put the Main Street Diner on the map, so the Bitch knows better than to refuse anything to a Clark.

Sometimes I think she's actually entertaining the fantasy that there could be something between Ten and me. Seriously. If she had some grip on reality she would see that I'm not his type at all. All the girls he dates are flat. They're the no-butt-no-breasts sort of girls, so androgynous looking you would not know they were female if you were standing behind them.

I'm just the opposite. There's nothing flat about me. I'm all curves. Objectively, I know I have a pretty face but the rest of me is not fashionably thin. I'm obviously not the flavor of the decade but I try to make peace with it. Furthermore, now that Ten's in college, he dates older girls. I'm the kid sister he's never had. We're buddies.

We ride Ten's Superglide to Manhattan and have lunch, his treat, at Rockefeller Center, looking at the enormous tree. We walk around Central Park and in the west village and go to a concert in the lower East side. I'm so excited, it's ridiculous! But then I seldom go anywhere so this is a real adventure. Manhattan is like a different universe. Even the food doesn't taste the same. I just look up at the Christmas lights and smile at Ten.

"Enough with this stupid Christmas spirit," he says with good humor, "there's this club on Bowery. Really exciting things are happening there. That's where we're going now."

He's so passionate about music. If it were not for his influence the only thing I would know about is what plays on the radio. That's not fair to our school music teacher. The poor man is trying to broaden our horizons. He started with Chinese opera and seriously, it was like torture. A few weeks later that Oriental fiasco, he introduced us to African drums and that was fun.

Anyway, I love soul, I enjoy pop music but I'm curious about other types of music and Ten's a walking musical dictionary. I tease him and ask him when he's finally going to admit that 10CC actually stands for Tennessee Charles Clark and that he wrote *I'm Not In Love*. He's insulted, that's way too mainstream for him!

As Ten parks the bike I look around and realize we're in a really crappy part of town. I'm happy I'm not here alone. I'm happier when I see there's a huge bouncer by the door. Ten asks this mountain of a guy to keep an eye on his ride. I wonder if the man's armed because the street boasts a few crazies talking to themselves or yelling at the world. One of them is ranting about Vietnam. A veteran, I guess. The poor soul seems to be haunted by ghosts. There are also bums sleeping off their poison of choice on the pavement despite the cold weather. I see empty bottles of beer and cheap liquor. Those men are different from the Long Island drunks we have. They seem more damaged. As I remove my helmet I try not to stare but I can't, it's a morbid fascination. It's difficult to tear my eyes from them but I finally do to thread my fingers through Ten's hair to repair the flat I-just-removed-my-helmet look.

Ten lets me do it and smiles back at me. I think he likes that I baby him a bit. His mom's a notch colder than mine. I never thought it possible before I met the woman. My mother's the Queen Bitch while Ten's mum is the Ice Queen.

When I'm done fixing his hair we walk in the club. It's dark and busy and loud. Ten walks through the crowd with ease. I hold on to his hand and follow in his wake until he decides we're close enough to the stage. He's doing this for me. He's six three so he could probably watch the stage from the other side of the room. He pulls me in front of him. I take one step and then I become star struck.

Actually I think Ten and I are both star struck. I freeze and Ten bumps into me. I turn around and see he's gawking at this guy standing on the dance floor a few steps ahead of us. He's like the modern version of a classical Greek god. He must be around Ten's age, somewhere in his early twenties, and he's built like Ten. He's tall, broad shoulders visible under a leather jacket, slim waist in 501 jeans, and biker's boots. Funny, Ten and he are dressed just the same. He also has the very same biker's flat hairdo that Ten and I wore a minute ago. The more I look at him the more I realize that they could be brothers with identical square jaws and chestnut hair, except that Greek God's eyes are a light shade of blue whereas Ten's are so dark they look black.

But there's a major difference between them. Ten's got this good-boy look that makes all respectable mature woman want him to date their daughters. Ten looks safe and reliable. Ten actually does make me feel protected. When I'm with him I don't think about most of the dangers of the world. Greek God is in a totally different league. I can tell just by looking at the way he's moving around that he's anything but safe. He's seductive danger. He's attractive trouble. He's hot as hell.

My heart rate has quickened to the pulse of the rock song played by the performing band. I put my hand on Ten's shoulder and stand on my toes to whisper yell in his ear, "I think I'm in love."

He smiles at me and bends to whisper yell in mine, "So am I. I love bad boys." He laughs looking at the expression of my face as I process his statement. "Come on, Lovey. Don't tell me you hadn't figured it out before. Surely you know I swing both ways," he laughs.

I shake my head and smile. Of course at one time I did have questions about his preferences. I had noticed him staring at some hulk that caught my eye but when he started dating his flat girls, I thought that when he looked at guys he was just being protective of me. I believed he was just keeping an eye on who I was checking out. Okay, so now I know better, he looked too because we like the same type of guys.

"Well I kind of suspected," I admit. I want to ask him why he did not come out to me earlier. Did he not trust me enough? As far as the rest of the world is concerned, I understand the pretense. I guess he dates girls but keeps the guys a secret because he fears his grandfather's reaction. He would probably be banished from the family circle if they knew.

Greek God stares at us, turns around and walks away. We both watch him. Ten stands right behind me and says, "I have no idea which way this guy swings but there was a bulge in his pants as he looked at us. I wonder who sprouted it."

I laugh. Boys! How was he able to spot the other guy's hard on while I never saw a thing? There's an easy answer to this question. I was looking at the guy's eyes while Ten's gaze went south of his face.

We dance. Well Ten dances and I kind of sway to the beat while the band plays. It's not my kind of music but it's not unbearable. Soon enough the winter cold is forgotten and I'm really warm. I think the place is getting so crowded it's raising the temperature a notch. "Can you get drinks in this place?" I yell. I'm getting really hot and sweaty!"

Ten yells back in my ear, "Ok, Lovey, save my spot, I'll be right back." He leaves me to get us some drinks. I'm waiting for him to get back when Greek God comes over to me. He says something but the music's so loud I can't make out his words.

I shake my head and make a hand gesture to indicate I have no clue what he just said. He wraps a hand around one of my arms and pulls me closer to him. I look up to his face and I'm lost. It takes all my willpower not to raise my free hand up to trace his jawline or the contour of his lips with the tip of my fingers. I want to touch such perfection to check that it's real. I think my heart has stopped and I can't do anything else but gaze into the deep sea of his eyes. He bends over to me and asks, "Lost your boy friend?"

I take it what he's really asking is, "Are you guys together?"

Let's not get too excited. The question can be understood one of two ways. One, he's into Ten and wondering where he's gone. Second, he's asking if the coast is clear because he's into me. Oh my god, I think he may be into me because his face stays so close to my ear even after he's finished talking. He closes his eyes and I think he's breathing me in. It's so hot when he does that. I think I'm melting. My bones are no longer solid and I almost lean into him for support. Could I have on him the effect that he has on me? I don't know the guy and I feel so pulled to him it's frightening. I steady myself and remember I have the power of speech. Conveniently I don't have to yell since he stayed bent over. His ear is next to my lips.

"My friend went to get us drinks."

He pulls up his face and does not even try to hide the smile from his face as he says, "So, he's just a friend."

I can't tear my eyes from the curve of his lips. Before I make a fool of myself, I'm saved by Ten's return. Greek God's face turns to him giving a chance to see how nicely etched a profile he has. This man is so perfect it's scary.

"Hi, I'm Alexander."

Ten smiles and says, "I'm Ten and I see you've met Lyv."

"Like Lyv Ullmann?"

I nod and I'm impressed. Most of the time I have to repeat my name and explain that, no, it's not short for anything else. It's just Lyv. My mother is an Ingmar Bergman groupie but saying this would be a stupid explanation since no one in my age group knows about the Swedish director and his star. Now Alexander's got a smug look on his face.

His hand is still on my arm and he pulls me closer to him. It's my turn to breathe him in. There's lavender and something else that could just be him. He looks tentatively at Ten as if asking permission for something. Ten raises his eyebrows and shrugs. I look back and forth between the two of them. Their silent communication baffles me. Those two did not know each other two minutes ago and they seem able to read each other's mind. I guess it's a guy thing.

The first band programmed for the evening show stops playing and the light brightens a bit. A bunch of guys get up on the stage to help pack up the gear of the exiting band and get the set ready for the next band. Ten and Alexander start a discussion about music. They seem to be on the same page from Blue Oyster Cult to ZZ Top. I listen to them without putting in my two cents. It's really not my type of music, I'm into mellow stuff. These days I listen to America but my two favorite songs are King Harvest's 'Dancing in the Moonlight' and Van Morrison's 'Moondance'. What can I say? I'm a moon girl.

Alexander's hand moves from my arm to my waist and it feels perfectly natural. It's like I belong nestled against him. Guys, probably the members of the next band to play, get on stage. The bass and the guitar players fine-tune several instruments. The drummer adjusts his seat and on his signal the lights get dim again. I watch them settling in until Alexander lets go of my waist and places a knuckle under my chin to turn my face to him. He brushes his lips against mine and says, "See you in a bit, Love."

I almost swoon as he walks away and climbs on to the stage as the band begins to play. It's not like he's the first guy that ever kissed me. I've done some more serious kissing activity a few times with boys at school but this light brush of our lips was something else. It was a tease and a promise of better things to come. Or not ... maybe it's all in my head.

He picks up a guitar from a stand and places himself in front of a mike. They play the intro to the song and he winks in my direction. A second later he opens his mouth and blows my mind away.

His voice is unlike any other I've ever heard. First it's smooth and velvety and sinfully tender when the band starts with a ballad. The lyrics are about sorrow and lost love. But then a hard rock piece follows and his voice turns raspy and angry. A voice like that could lead a revolution and bring a crowd to riot. Then there's a happy sexy love song and I want to be the one he sings about. Hell, I look around and everyone is in love with him. His stage presence is magical. They do five songs and when they stop the entire audience goes wild.

They do one more but no further encore despite our cheering. I guess it's because the club has a busy schedule for the night. The crew reappears to get everything ready for the next band while Alexander and his guys walk away back stage.

"I think a star is born," Ten says to me. "And the star has the hots for you my little Lovey."

I grin. Yep, he did kind of kiss me. It was sweet but I don't want to get my hopes up because... because I'm so insecure I can't believe someone like him could fall for me.

We hang around for a while listening to another band and Ten gets us another drink. We dance to a few of the songs of the third band but my heart is no longer in it. I'm crestfallen because Alexander does not come back. I try to hide it but Ten sees right through me.

"You wanna call it a night?" he asks.

"Yep, let's go."

We step out of the club and Ten tips the bouncer who's kept an eye on his precious baby. The man thanks him and jokes, "Can you tell which one is yours?"

Ten and I turn around and understand the question. Now that there are a few less motorcycle parked, we can see two perfectly identical Superglide bikes on the street.

Ten smiles and admits, "Nope, without looking at the license plate I can't."

"The one on the left is yours, the one on the right belongs to Xander. He's one of the regulars who's playing tonight. When I saw you I thought you were his cosmic brother, dude. You look like him, you dress like him and you have the same bike."

I don't know about cosmic brothers but I do know they now have something more in common. The two of them have found their way under my skin.

Chapter 2

I t's eleven. I'm late. My shift is starting and I'm still a ten minutes walk away. It's Saturday, one of the busiest days and the Bitch is going to kill me.

I want to throw my bicycle into a ditch, sit down, and cry. The chain has derailed again and I can't seem to fix it properly. My hands are covered with black greasy goo. I'm sure I've put some on my face as well.

Today I hate my life. I hate my lousy high school, I hate the Christmas holidays, I hate my shitty family, and above all I hate my crappy self. I take a deep breath and plow ahead dragging the stupid thing along. Maybe when I'm calmer I'll find a way to fix it again.

I'm in a tunnel. I've been living in a tunnel forever and I can't wait for my life to begin. I want to run away and start living. I could do that now but I know it's harder to get ahead in life without a minimum of education. So I need to finish high school. If I don't I'll never be able to go to college. I've never talked about my dreams with my family. I know better than that.

"Don't let your grades go to your head, Lyv," the Bitch always says. "You're 'As' are nothing more than evidence of the mediocrity of the American education system."

I gave up on her a long time ago. I've let go of hope about my father as well. He's just an empty shell. Some days I look deep into his eyes for a glimmer, but no. No one is living inside the wimp. I wonder if there ever was someone in there. He's her yes-man and he must like it that way. If he didn't he'd do something to change it, right?

They're more keepers than parents. Well keeper's not the right word. Hell, I've been earning my keep for years now. I've been doing more than my share of chores around the house and I've worked way too many hours at the diner.

I don't even score minimum wage because the Bitch thinks she owns me. She's got me so brainwashed I have to remind myself time and time again that I'm my own person and that no one owns me, especially not her. I've only started keeping my tips since last summer. I think I shamed her into it when I refused James Clark's tip one Sunday morning.

"What's wrong with you kid?" he had asked. "My money's not good enough for you?"

"I'm sorry Sir," I had said. "I did not mean to insult you. It's just that my mother does not allow me to keep my tips..."

I don't know what the old man told the Bitch but since then she stopped confiscating my tips and I've been stashing money away. It's my run-away ticket. I'm not about to spend it on a bicycle. If the Bitch wants me to get to work on time she's going to have to do something about it.

Until last week I just hated everything about my life. Everything but Ten. Now I hate myself too. I can't seem to get Alexander out of my head. He's in my dreams every single night. When I wake up I'm a mess and I realize how lost I am. How did I let this guy I don't know get into my head like that? The Bitch may be right after all. I really am as dumb as dirt. When Alexander brushed his lips to mine, for a second, I saw a light at the end of my tunnel. Now I know it was nothing more than a runaway train coming to hit me full blast. I kick a rock on the road and curse out loud.

A pick up truck slows down behind me on the road and the drivers calls out, "Hey Lyv, need a lift?" It's Dave, the father of a girl in my class and the owner of the local garage.

"Yes. Thanks, Dave." There's no need to force a smile onto my face. The man is my savior today. Again.

He stops the truck and I throw my bicycle in the back. I climb in and find the rag he usually has on the passenger seat. I use it to wipe my hands as well as I can.

"Your chain again." It's not a question. He knows. We've played this scene before. It's not the first time he's picked me up on my way to work.

"I'll look at it and see what I can do." I think he wants to add something but he thinks better of it. He's wise enough to know to mind his own business. Our town is way too small in the winter to meddle in other people's lives. I think many of our neighbors would do something if they saw traces of physical abuse on me but she only leaves emotional scars. Since those are not clearly visible, the neighbors keep to themselves.

"Thank you Dave. I really appreciate this."

He winks and jokes. "You know me, anything for a few extra pancakes."

"You're on. Anytime." The man's got a sweet tooth and extra pancakes are the only way he lets me pay him back for his trouble.

Pam's so lucky to have a father who's nice. He looks at me and smiles. Oops, I think I must have said it out loud. It happens to me way too often. The thoughts that cross my mind find their way out past my lips. At least today it's not embarrassing. Uncomfortable but not embarrassing.

I wish I had scored a father like that, an affectionate man who truly believed part of his purpose in life is to take good care of his kids. I think it's watching him interact with his daughter that made me realize that something was really wrong with my parents. He's so sweet I can't help envy Pam.

"There we are young lady," he says as he stops the truck in front of the diner. "Come by at the end of your shift."

"Thank you Dave."

"Stop it, Lyv. You're sounding like a broken record." I get down from the truck and laugh. He's right, I've not stopped thanking the man since he picked me up.

He drives away and as I cross the street to get to work, I concentrate on the positive aspect of the day. I broke down but it did not rain. Actually the weather's glorious and not too cold so I did not freeze and then I did not have to walk all the way... and Ten's bike is parked in front of my work place. I'm happy he's here but I still feel like crap. He's my ray of sunshine. The rest of my life sucks big time.

I walk into the diner and as my eyes adjust to the change in light I spot Ten. He's in a booth facing the door and he waves at me as I come in. My mother is a few steps behind him, she's taking the order of the patrons in the adjacent booth. She glares at me.

I raise my hands to show how dirty they are and walk straight in the kitchen. If I'm gonna catch hell, I'd rather be yelled at in the relative privacy of the kitchen while I wash my hands. I'll kill two birds with one stone.

I take a bowl and mix dish washing liquid and raw sugar. That's my magical paste to fight bicycle grease. The cook looks at me and says, "You got some on your face too, Honey."

"Where?"

"Let me do this," Martha dips a finger in the bowl and scrubs the top of my ear and my forehead. She's a little rough around the edges but I guess that's why she's managed to stay around here so long while the rest of the help quits at the end of each season. Martha's always good to me and all her gestures go straight to my heart.

It's pitiful to crave attention so much.

"Here, you're good to go. I think there's some in your hair but black on black no one can tell." She frowns a bit and adds, "You'd better get cracking. Your mama, Honey, she's in a foul mood."

"Thanks Martha." While I wipe my hands, she goes and gets me my apron. "Any particular reason aside from my being late?"

She checks that I have an order pad and a pen in the front pocket and says, "Yeah, Baby Girl. The Clark boy's refusing to order from anyone else but you. She's playing along as if it's fine but I can tell she's pissed."

Thank you, Ten, for feeding fuel to her fire. He could have done it on purpose to spite her. Ten's funny that way. He thinks negative attention is better than no attention at all. I told him I would swap the Ice Queen's indifference for the Bitch's constant wrath in a heartbeat but he claims it's worse to be ignored. He has no clue. I would so appreciate being ignored for a while!

The most ironic thing is that our mothers brought us together. Well the despair they created in us did. Ten and I met on Christmas day at the very end of the fishing pier. I'm not certain that I would have jumped into the icy choppy ocean that day but I don't contradict him when he says we saved each other's lives. We probably did.

I refrain from the impulse of putting my hand in my hair to smooth it. If there's bicycle grease in there, I don't want to put it back on my hands. Martha ties my apron and I walk out of the kitchen just as the Bitch enters with the new order.

"Good morning mother," I say as I rush away.

I walk to Ten's booth and say, "May I take your order, sir?" My tone is formal but there's a big smile on my face. My smile freezes and my heart starts pounding in my chest. He's not alone in the booth.

"Look who I rode in with," Ten says.

Alexander's here. A thousand questions collide in my mind. How did they hook up again? Who's idea was it to come here? Is he here for me or are they together and I read him wrong?

"Are you not happy to see me?" Alexander asks. There's a look of genuine concern on his face.

"Yes." He raises his eyebrows. "No. Shit, your question is all twisted. It's yes, I'm happy to see you. It's just, you know, I'm surprised to see you here, in my own little hell corner."

"Well, how else was I going to see you again?"

Ten coughs to catch my attention. My mother's coming our way. I put my work face back on and flip the pages of Alexander's menu as if we had been talking about his order, "So we have a very nice special for brunch..." Alexander does not look too surprised by my sudden change of tone. I guess Ten must have briefed him on the fact that the Bitch and I don't get along.

Ten cuts me short, "Lovey, don't bother, we've decided. We'll both be having scrambled eggs and a bagel with lox and cream cheese."

"I'll bring your order to the kitchen and will be right out

with your coffee," I say and rush away while Ten starts chatting up my mother.

"Mrs. Wild," he says. "Would it be okay if I took Lyv out tonight after her shift?"

I can't make out her answer but I recognize the sugary voice she takes when she wants to be seductive. I place the order with Martha in the kitchen, greet new clients, and get them settled in.

I bring coffee to my boys. Funny how I think of them as *my boys*. I like that. They both take it black. No sugar no cream. "So what did the Bitch say?" I ask Ten.

Alexander gasps. I look at him. He seems genuinely shocked. I shrug and let it slide. I know my nickname for my mother can come as a surprise when you don't know her but when you do, you think it's kind of tame. When I was a kid it was Cruella. I've grown up. So has her spitefulness, hence my name for her. I still don't know why she's so mean to me. If she did not want me, why didn't she just abandon me instead of torturing me everyday?

Ten answers my question, "She said we had to bring you home early because you've got the opening shift tomorrow."

I frown. No I don't. I swapped with Wendy. She took my Sunday morning in exchange for her New Year's day. Her husband does not work that day and she's prepared a special day to celebrate his third month of sobriety. Did that get messed up? It makes no difference to me but yet I feel sorry for her.

"Good," I say. "I get out at 5 but I have to go to Dave to see if he was able to fix my bicycle."

"We'll be there," Ten and Alexander say together. They laugh and hit a high five. I giggle as I walk away. Boys!

Chapter 3

I step out of the diner shortly after five and Alexander is sitting on his bike parked across the street. He's holding a couple of helmets. He puts his on as I walk to him.

"I would love to kiss you, Love," he says looking behind me as he hands me a helmet,"but Ten said it would be a bad idea to have any display of affection in front of your mother."

I really like that he calls me Love. I look inside the helmet. There's a wind-breaker jacket. A nice thought, I won't freeze. I turn around as I put it on. Sure enough, the Bitch is standing by the door. She's been bugging me all day to find out who Ten was with and I played dumb. I said he was just a friend of Ten's. I don't tell her more. It's just damage control. The less she knows the less she can hurt me.

I climb on the bike behind Alexander and strap the helmet on my head. I sit up straight with my hands on my knees until we turn a corner. Only then do I relax and lean against Alexander's back wrapping my arms around him.

"That's much better," he says.

I close my eyes and breathe in. There's the smell of his leather jacket plus his touch of lavender in the crisp winter air. It smells like freedom. I imagine running away with him, riding out in the sun on the open road and living in the moment. The Doors' 'Riders On the Storm' plays softly in my head for a few seconds and then the record crashes as I remember my bicycle. I stiffen up and Alexander slows down and asks.

"What now, Love?" I adore my new nickname.

"I forgot about my bicycle."

"Ten took care of it," he says and speeds up making conversation impossible. I know the road we're on. It's the way to the Clark's estate. Alexander gets to the gate and fits a key in the automatic portal mechanism. The massive wrought iron gates slide open and we drive in on the gravel road that cuts through the manicured lawn. We pass the main building all the way to Ten's beach bungalow.

It's a tiny construction on stilts and it has survived a few heavy storms. James Clark had it refurbished when Ten turned 18. He thought his grandson needed some privacy. I've always been suspicious of such generosity. Sometimes I wonder if James does not use it with his conquests-he calls them his twinkies-when Ten's in the city. But that may just be my very naughty imagination.

I get off the bike, remove my helmet and fold my windbreaker while Alexander parks in the sheltered corner under the building. It's where Ten usually parks. Alexander takes another key out of his pocket and opens the door for us. It hits me. Ten's not here. We're going to be alone.

I'm elated and I'm terrified. I act cool as I walk up the steps and in the bungalow. It's a safe place. It's familiar. Instead of turning the lights on, I flip the electrical shutter switch. The metal shutters roll up noisily as Alexander locks the door behind us.

We're alone, completely private. I've been dreaming about this every night for a week. In my dream the setting was blurry. I realize I'm a bit crazy. I'm here, all alone with this guy I barely know and instead of being frightened I'm ... what am I? I'm not sure but probably not as wary as I should be!

I look out through the window. The ocean view from the small deck of the bungalow is glorious. It's a south exposure. Perfect for dawn and dusk. However I'm not thinking about the color of the sky right now. I'm noticing that the deck has been set up for us. I'm sure it's Ten's work. He's hooked up the large hammock he sleeps on in the summer and set a table next to it. There's a hurricane lamp and a picnic basket on the table as well as a few warm looking covers.

Ten's good with stuff like that. When we go out for a picnic there's never anything missing. I smile inwardly thinking that he's so thorough, I have no doubt there're condoms in the basket just in case I decide that Alexander should be the one... Yep, Ten's a regular boy scout.

Alexander stands behind me with his hands on my hips and kisses my neck. I can hardly think anymore. My impulse is to let go and lean it to him. I so want to live in the moment. But I can't. My mind is reeling. I've been slapped by the Bitch too many times to let my defenses down without some sort of struggle. So I brace myself and say, "I have questions."

There may be too much bite in my tone but the tone of his answer his sweet. "Fair enough. What do you want to know?"

"How did you find me?"

"Oh, that was easy. I tipped the bouncer. He's got a weird type of memory. He says it's like a slide show he can play in his head looking at the details of each picture. He had looked hard enough at Ten's bike to memorize its license plate. He just closed his eyes and gave me the number. It was kind of spooky when he did that. Anyway, I called my brother Andrew. He's a cop. I gave him the license plate and I got Ten's address. I drove there-posh building by the way-left a message with his doorman, and he called me the very same day."

He turns me around and brings me closer to him. I rest my head on his chest. He's unzipped his jacket and I can slide my arms underneath and soak up his warmth. I breathe him in again. I love the way he smells, it's intoxicating but not enough to forget my questions.

"Why me?" I didn't mean to let that question out but I couldn't help myself.

There's nothing special about me. Despite what the Bitch has been telling me, I know my face is cute but that's all I have. She has a point when she says that I'm not worth a second glance. I'm short and big. There's nothing special about my brown eyes and my hair is blah. I'm definitely not in the same league as Alexander.

"You have no idea how lovely you are," he says. "I just saw you and I knew. First I knew that I just wanted you. I had this plan to seduce you after the show but then I got stuck back stage. When I managed to get away you had left." He stops for a while as if looking for his words. "A couple of days later I realized there was more. More than I had guessed at first. I could not stop thinking about you."

"Because I was the one that got away?"

"There's probably some of that." He chuckles and kisses my forehead. "There's also the fact that there is something irresistible about you. And then I love that you liked me before you heard me sing and you had no clue who I was."

I look up to him and ask, "Why? Did I miss something? Are you famous?"

"Well kind of. I'm underground famous if that makes any sense." He laughs. "In the music industry, I'm the flavor of the month. There've been articles about me in the press and two majors are offering me record deals," his expression is proud and wary at the same time.

I recognize the look on his face. It's the look of someone who's accomplished something and can't rejoice for fear it's going to vanish in a second if he does. I've seen it on Ten's face when he's aced something and he waits for his mother to acknowledge him. I can't resist the urge to comfort Alexander just as I can't resist the urge to comfort Ten when I watch him miss his mother's approval.

"You should not feel like you're walking on thin ice." He stiffens up, like I just overstepped. I continue anyway. "You should have no doubt about your career. You're going to be a huge star. You have this splendid voice and your stage presence is ... hot, amazing, fabulous."

"Yep, I'm a regular teenager heart-throb," he says with a light tone.

"Hey, don't knock teenagers. They buy records. They go to concerts. They're going to be your bread and butter."

"Talking of bread and butter," he says, "Are you hungry? I'm famished. I can't wait to see what Ten has hidden in that basket."

He opens the sliding door and pulls me behind him on the deck. He picks me up as if I weigh nothing and drops me in the hammock. "I can't believe you just did that! I'm no lightweight. You make me feel sexy and fragile. I love it." I gag the independent woman I plan to become one day and tell her we'll discuss this later. Right now is not the time for protests.

Alexander lights the lamp, grabs the covers and jumps in the hammock next to me. "You are beautiful just the way you are. Curves are sexy."

I spread the covers on us and snuggle next to him, my head on his shoulder. It's so strange. It's the first time I'm in bed with a guy-well, almost in bed-and it does not feel awkward at all. He's so handsome I can't believe he wants me. I know he does because he's actually looked for me and found me. I need to pinch myself, or better yet, I need to touch him.

I can't wait for him to kiss me. I mean a real kiss, not the sweet brush on the lips I was treated to in the club. I sigh. Yes. I want a movie type kiss that will leave me out of breath.

"Oh you do now?" He's smiling.

Here I go again. I guess I did say that out loud. Somehow his gaze on my lips make me forget how embarrassing this defect of mine is. He seems amused by my bluntness and says, "I think that can be arranged."

He pulls me towards him and scoots down a little so that we are both on our side, face to face. His eyes are on my mouth. His face hovers very close to mine. He freezes there for an instant and then our eyes lock. I'm holding my breath but not closing my eyes. Neither does he as he closes in and somehow merges with me.

As our lips meet, there is not a solid part left in my body. I have melted to fit snuggly against him. He's this other part of me that I did not know was missing before. I'm still breathing but I'm not sure it's necessary. Fitting into him is all that I need to exist, to be me. After a moment I cannot measure he pulls away and kisses the tip of my nose. I sigh and shiver.

"Are you cold, Love?" He's tone is so tender it brings tears to my eyes. God, I crave him and his affection so badly that it's almost too much for me. I shake my head and then burrow against him and hold on for dear life. He holds me tightly and whispers in my ear that I'm safe with him and he's not going anywhere. One arm is wrapped around me and his free hand caresses my hair.

"How was your day after we left?" he asks.

"Just fine, it's quiet this time of year," I tell him. "The busy season starts in the spring."

"So what do you do for fun? What do you love doing? I want to know more about you."

I don't know what to say. The fact is that I go to school, do my homework and work at the diner. I have a very light social life since most of the girls in school have given up on me. It's not that they don't like me, I actually think they do, probably because I'm a great listener. They have given up because I can only hang out with them during lunch recess and around the school library when we have a group project to work on. Actually the only thing fun I've done in the past years have involved being isolated with a boy in a deserted section of the library and I'm not about to explain that to Alexander.

"I don't really do anything fun except hang out with Ten," I tell him. "Between school and work, I don't have that much time."

He kisses me again and then says, "I don't usually do the tender bit."

I lift my head and look at him. "What do you mean?"

He shrugs, "I'm a get them and leave them the next day type of guy."

"You are?" There's such a discrepancy between his words and his attitude that I'm unsettled.

"But that's not who I want to be with you, Love." He closes his eyes as if what he was about to say was painful. "I don't know why, but I want you to need me. It does not make sense but I'm not fighting it."

What he's saying is so perfect, the tears come back to my eyes. I blink and he wipes them away with his thumb. "Those are happy tears," I tell him. "Right now, here with you, I feel something I've never felt before. I feel at home."

Chapter 4

I n my dream my bed is rocking; gently but it is rocking. Actually someone is nudging my shoulder. I open my eyes. I'm not in bed. I'm in a hammock and in Alexander's arms. Ten is standing next to us, on the deck of his bungalow. He points an index to his wristwatch and then puts three fingers up.

Wow, it's three a.m. I have to open the diner at 8, which means I have to get there at 7. But first I need to go back home, shower, change, and then get to work.

As long as I get to work in time the Bitch will probably avoid asking any questions about what I did and what time I got in. Past ten or eleven P.M. at the most, she's too drunk to remember a thing anyway.

Shit, how will I get to work? I don't even have a bicycle anymore.

Before I go in panic mode, I hand signal Ten to come to my side and help me get out of the hammock without flipping the entire contraption upside down. We have this very basic secret silent language that we created when we were kids that we keep using every so often just for the fun of it. Today it's proving really handy.

He walks to my side, picks me up and sets me down on my feet. The wood is cold underneath my toes. I have to find the shoes I kicked down to the floor earlier. Before I do that I lean over and wrap the covers around Alexander. Incredibly, he's even more handsome when he sleeps. His smile is almost angelic. All his anxieties appear to vanish as he rests. I wish I could look so serene but I'm pretty sure I don't since most mornings I wake up with clenched jaws. Alexander stirs a little and opens his eyes. He looks up to me and then sees Ten.

"I'm taking her home," Ten says. "Better me than you in case her mother's still up. I'll be back in a little while."

"Goodbye, Love," Alexander says sleepily. "See you soon."

I blow him a kiss while I slide my feet in my shoes and follow Ten into the bungalow where he picks up the windbreaker and the helmet from where I left them on the way in. We go down the steps and I'm about to go to the bike by the fence when I remember it's not his, it's Alexander's. I follow Ten to his bike.

It's parked on the gravel path that leads back to the main road. When I feel we're far enough to speak without being heard by Alexander I catch Ten's arm and hug him.

"Thank you, so much. It's the best Christmas present I ever had!"

He's grinning and looking mighty proud of himself. He can be. He's made me the happiest girl on earth tonight. "And you have another one waiting for you at your house, Lovey" he says.

"I do?"

"Yep, I found you a bicycle."

"What do you mean you *found* me a bicycle." I badly need a ride but I also badly need to keep some pride.

"Well my mother got this new 10 speed monster for Christmas so you're getting the old one that would otherwise rust away in the garage."

He looks at me with a cocky smile tilting his head as he zips up my windbreaker. He knew I would not let him get me a bicycle so he got one for the Ice Queen instead.

This is perfect. The Bitch will be happy that I have some means of transportation again to get to school and to work and since it's a used bicycle I could always say that I purchased it.

"You know I love you don't you?" I say.

"Yes I do but I've bet you've said that to all the guys you've seen tonight," he jokes.

"Nope, you're the only one," I protest. "He may have chipped a bit of my heart but I'm not sure I want him to know it yet."

Ten climbs on the bike and says, "Poor man, don't you see how hard he's fallen for you?"

I climb behind him, "You really think so?"

We start moving as Ten says, "Only time will tell but if I were a betting man, I'd put good money on him."

I so hope he's right and that Alexander will hang around for a while. Ten drives me home and sure enough, there's this lovely bicycle by the garage door where I usually tie mine.

"What time do you finish your shift?" he asks.

"Right after lunch."

"Good, we'll be there." I watch him ride away smiling. My life does not suck that much after all. I take a quick shower, sleep a couple of hours, and get to work.

We're drawing a big crowd today. Many people are taking a four day weekend and spending Christmas in the Hamptons with their family. The entire Clark clan plus Alexander show up at eleven for brunch.

James Junior arrives first on foot. Ten's father likes to walk. When Ten was a teenager he used to walk all the way here with him. I thought they had some quality time together but I guess I was wrong because it stopped the day Ten got his bike.

Then James Senior arrives with his daughter, Carla, and her son who's also called James. Since three James at the same table would be a bit confusing, James Clark Evans, Carla's son, goes by the name of Jimmy. He's with his buddy Steven. Those two are attached the hip. They do everything together. Ten even hinted that they share their girlfriends and that sent my mind in a spin. I wonder how that works. The questions I have pop in my mind every single time I see them and I'm pretty sure I blush. They must think I have a crush on one of them... or on both of them.

Last there's Alexandra Clark, Ten's mother, aka the Ice Queen, with her latest guru. He's her yoga master who has replaced the Tai Chi instructor who previously replaced the meditation whatever. At least her latest obsessions are keeping her in shape. Last year she was into less physical stuff. She was searching for the meaning of life through astrology and numerology. Obviously neither her husband nor her son, nor the family money, are giving any meaning to her life.

The two women have tea, no sugar, no milk and half a grapefruit. Between them it's a competition. The winner is the one who eats the least. Their idea of a splurge is a bite of toast. I hope for them they enjoy looking so thin as much as I enjoy eating.

The men on the other hand are serious customers. They pile up the pancakes, the muffins, the eggs, and the hash. When they're done, James Senior walks by the kitchen to thank Martha. He flirts with her and it's cute. Martha blushes like a young girl when he does. I like the old man. Even though he has created an empire, James Senior is still a carpenter at heart and a very simple man with healthy values.

James Junior, on the other hand is a real snob. That probably explains his choice of spouse. Through the years, he's persistently questioned my friendship with Ten. He's told his son countless times that to get ahead in life he should stop hanging out with the help. Lately he's stopped. His son's officially dating proper society girls in college so it's okay if he slums with me when he's at the beach house.

The fact that Ten became financially independent when his grandmother died may also have helped. Ten's inherited a four bedroom apartment in Manhattan from his beloved Granny and the rent he collects from his roommates pays for the maintenance and his living expenses. I'm sure that given the choice he would trade his freedom for a little more time with Granny. She gave him the attention he craved so much when he spent the summers with her. She was the sweetest woman. I really liked her a lot and I think she liked me too.

Slowly the diner empties until there's just Ten and Alexander at one table and our regular in-house aspiring author nursing a coffee and scribbling away furiously in one booth. I've cleaned all the tables, checked with Martha to see if she needed anything from me. Wendy just walked in. I'm almost ready to go.

Before I check out, I go refresh the author's cup. "Hey Pulitzer, you seem inspired today," I say as I give him a refill. He looks up from his notebook and grins at me. "Anything else I can get you before I finish my shift?"

"No, I'm fine my dear, run along, it seems you're going to have an interesting day." I raise my eyebrows showing that I have no clue what he's talking about.

"I know, I should mind my own business but I couldn't help but notice the dragon's not around and you've got two knights in shining armor waiting for you. Life is looking good for you, Princess." I giggle looking at my two knights.

"It's the same story that's told over and over again,"

he says. "They've swapped white stallions for shiny bikes but nothing's new under the sun."

"I like the romantic way you look at life," I tell him. "I can't wait to read your novel and see what sitting in this place every day has inspired you with."

"Oh you will young lady, you will."

He dives back into his own world and I go through the kitchen to the little room that serves as storage and locker room to check on Wendy who is about to start her shift. She just walked in and looks a mess.

"What's up my girl?" I ask but just looking at her I know the answer. She's had another fight with her husband and whatever plans she had for New Year's day, she's given up on. It must be bad if she'd rather spend the first day of the year working than hanging around with him on his day off.

"He's drinking again," she says and shrugs her shoulders. "I figured that since I was not going to do anything on my New Year's day, you should get it back and maybe do something fun with Ten if the Bitch lets you get away."

"I'm so sorry, Honey," I say. She's a tiny little thing. She must be about my height five two or maybe five three but she's so frail that when you look at her you think a strong wind could blow her away. We have each other's back at work but at home there's nothing

I can do for her. I go to hug her and I notice she's wincing. "Did he hit you again?"

"No I ran out and I tripped," she answers sheepishly.

I don't believe her for a second but I let it slide because now is not the time and place to badger her about standing up for herself. I'm telling myself that it's her life, it's her choice and I really should not interfere. I've got enough to do with my own life not to meddle with hers. What do I know about being in love with a drunk? Probably more than I'm willing to admit. After all at some point, way back when, I must have loved my drunk of a mother.

I take the coward's way out and run to meet Ten and Alexander. I walk back into the dining area and watch them talking to each other animatedly. I'm happy they get along so well. I love it when the people I care about like each other.

I feel a gaze on me and see that Pulitzer is watching me intently. I make a mental note. Later this week I need to ask him what his pen name is and what his book is about.

The guys get up as I come back to them. They look so much alike it's uncanny. They both have this sort of grace as they move their long bodies. There's something feline about them. "Are you ready?" Ten asks.

"Sure, let's get this show on the road," I say. The three of us walk out and as I strap my helmet on I realize have a choice of ride.

As if reading my mind, Ten choses for me and tells me, "Ride with him, Lovey." I hop on the saddle behind Alexander and off we go.

Alexander, Ten and I are lying on our backs on a large blanket on the beach in front of the bungalow. That's where Ten and I usually hang out. It's not legally a private beach but people have to walk for such a long time from the road to get there that we seldom have company in the winter. The sun is out and the clouds few and far between. I'm in between the two of them listening to Alexander telling us about the two record deals he's been offered. The most interesting one comes with a one-year tour as the first act of some well established bands of the label.

"That's why I was really excited about this offer when I got it," Alexander says.

"You're not anymore? What made you change your mind?" Ten asks.

"Oh, I didn't. I'm going. I've worked too hard to get where I am today to give anything up but there's this gal I just met and ..." he does not finish his sentence but flips to his side and looks at me. "Now that I've found her, I realize I'm not going to like being away from her so much. She may have too much time on her hands."

I'm not sure how to feel about this. What we have is so new. Does he think I'm so fickle that I could not wait for him while he tours? Now on the other hand, I realize I should be worried. A year is a very long time.

"Yes it is," he says, and I realize that I must have said it out loud

"It can seem like an eternity." I add.

Always practical Ten asks, "Did you get a copy of the schedule? I'm pretty sure they can't have the bands and crew working every single night for a year. There's gotta be gaps in the tour schedule to let every one go home every so often."

"You're probably right," Alexander says. "I had not thought about that."

"So take this deal that works best for you," I tell him while what I really want to say is, *please don't go*. I suck it up and say, "I'm not going anywhere. If anyone should be worried about your touring for a year, it's me."

"Why?" He seems genuinely surprised by my answer.

"You'll be the one subjected to temptation," I answer. "You're going to become a huge success, you'll have groupies throwing themselves at you... some of them will surely be very pretty and very persuasive and you'll probably not always be strong enough to resist temptation."

Ten laughs and cuts me off. "Listen, Lovey, I don't want to sound like the arrogant bastard that I can be, but I'm pretty sure that Alexander's like me. Tour or no tour, he can get a different lay every night if he wants to, so that's really not the problem."

"You're probably right," I admit. I turn my head to look in Alexander's eyes and he says,

"We're going to have to figure out a way to trust each other. Can you think of anything that I could do right now to convince you that I'm serious about you?"

Staring at the sky again, I ponder about it for an instant before answering him. "No. I can't. I'll think about it though."

"Knowing her, you're gonna have to stick around for the next ten years before she stops doubting you really care about her," Ten jokes. "That's about how long it took me."

I send a friendly punch to his shoulder in mock anger. Ten calls to Alexander, "Hey man! Hold your woman. She's dangerous."

It's cute the way Ten called me Alexander's woman and it's hot that Alexander didn't object. Alexander rolls me over so that I face him and kisses me. I wrap my arms around him and hold on tight to him. When we come back for air, I say, "So you'll be gone on tour for a year."

"Yes, I will. Let's go back in so I can get warmer before I hit the road," Alexander says.

"You're going back now?" I ask not hiding my disappointment.

"Yes, I need to work every so often and my uncle's bar is the best job I could find. He's flexible with my schedule and the tips are great but I still need to get there to earn my pay. Don't fret, Love, I'm coming back next weekend to start the New Year with you."

"Cool," I say.

After Alexander goes, Ten and I stay together a bit. "Next week, we'll have the house to ourselves," Ten tells me. "My parents have this big to-do in the city and Grandpa is flying away to Acapulco with Carla and Jimmy."

"Weren't you supposed to go with them this year?"

"Right, I was but I changed my mind. I think I've found something more fun to do."

"What's that?"

"Being happy," he says and gives me a dreamy smile.

"Did you meet someone too?"

"Yes I did."

"I'm happy for you. Tell me about him!" I smile at Ten. My friend's happy and today, I'm officially the luckiest girl on earth.

"Nope, he's still officially a mystery date. You'll just have to make something up in your head, but whatever you dream up, it won't be anything like the real thing."

"Oh, come on, tell me just a little bit about him. Just a rough description, just two words and I'll let my imagination fill in the blanks."

"Well, if you insist," Ten says. He thinks about it and then gives me two words "Italian. Model."

"Wow, good choice of word. You've just spurred my imagination!"

Chapter 5

This has been the longest week of my life. Since I kissed Alexander goodbye on Sunday, I've been counting down the days and then the hours and now the minutes before his return. The clock has been ticking slower every day.

I've been working at the diner and doing all the assignments we have for next week when classes will start again after the holidays. When I was done with that and the house chores I even found time to lay on my bed and daydream about the future. I want to major in science. I dream about nursing school and on good days I have medical school fantasies but my bubble bursts as soon as I try to think about the logistics of it. College is going to be hard enough to finance.

I've finished my shift early and I'm standing across the street from the diner waiting for Alexander or Ten to come pick me up. Traffic is slow and every single engine sound I hear has me standing on my toes.

The Bitch is standing by the door looking at me suspiciously. I wish there were more work and patrons to keep her busy but then again that wouldn't be good. She would use it as an excuse to keep me from going. She's noticed that something has changed.

Pullitzer asked her if I was going to a party for New Year's Eve and the Bitch answered "Yes, for the first time she got an invitation. You know fat girls are not so popular. So of course I said she could go." Anything to make herself look good. Naturally, she said it loud enough for me to hear. I let her nasty comments slide and actually smiled at her. That threw her and made my day.

The fact of the matter is that when I smiled, I was not really thinking about what she was saying. I was recalling a phone conversation I had with Alexander one night at Ten's place. Alexander called just as Ten had finished giving me a motorcycle riding lesson. I've been riding for a while but Ten wants my transitions to be smoother. I was telling Alexander that it felt strange to be in the driver's part of the saddle with Ten right behind me when he said that he could never have done it. Something about being so close to me in that position would have been too distracting.

"But you can concentrate when I'm behind you," I had said. "So what's the difference?"

"Oh the innocence of a sweet little virgin," was his answer.

I guess I'm really innocent because before Alexander I had never let a guy hold me as tight as he has. But then I had never felt the desire to do so.

I snap out of my daydreaming as a bike turns the corner. It's Ten. He waves at the Bitch with a big smile on his face. I know he's right, he's gotta keep on her good side otherwise she would lock me up in my room and physically bar access from the house during the rest of the holidays. Still, when he does that I want to strangle him. I look away from the door and decide that I will not let any thought of her spoil my fun. I hop on behind Ten and instead of going in the direction of his place, he goes for a U turn. I lean over and ask "Where are we going?"

"Your place, you'll need a bathing suit, I turned on the hot tub."

"Oh" is all I manage to say as I come to terms with the fact that I'm going to see Alexander almost naked. That's exciting but then it dawns on me that he's going to see parts of me that are way to round to be fashionable.

A vision of Twiggy in The Boy Friend comes to my mind and I chase her away with a light broom. I breathe in deeply and tell myself that there's no way Alexander could have missed that I'm no lightweight. Seriously, he even lifted me up to put me on the hammock so he can't ignore my size. But it's one thing to kind of feel it or even guess the shapes I hide under my baggy clothes and quite another to see all of me. What will I do if he changes his mind? What will I do if he runs? What will I do... as I get to the house, I tune out all of the nasty comments the Bitch makes about my weight, except for this one. Her favorite one for patrons of the diner is, "No, I don't have Jello on the menu. I wouldn't let my daughter serve food that wiggles just like she does."

I run to my room to find my suit and she's back in my head. "Have you seen the size of you? You're like a double wide ... I'm surprised they make swimming suits for people like you. I wouldn't think there's a market for it. People that big should have the good sense to hide."

My room is a mess. I left for work an hour earlier than my mother. She had plenty of time to toss it. What was she looking for? I know I'm not entitled to any privacy. As far as she's concerned I'm not entitled to anything. I know better than to put anything in writing that I would not want her to read or to keep any telling memento of anything. Still I hate it when she does this because I need to spend an hour putting everything back in place.

The clothes are no problem. My wardrobe is so limited it takes all of three minutes to get all my stuff back in the drawers. It's the school stuff that rattles me. She opens the binders and then tosses everything to the floor. I so hate the Bitch. I leave as much stuff as I can in my locker at school and put numbers on my loose binder pages so I can put them back together more quickly but still, it pisses me off. I guess as long as it does she'll keep on doing it.

I breathe in deeply, grab the suit, and then get out leaving the room as is. It will wait. I rush back to Ten and my hours of freedom. Alexander will be staying at Ten's place until the first. We're going to have a New Year's celebration.

I deserve a celebration since the Bitch made me skip Christmas all together this year. I guess staying alone that night was better than sitting with her, watching her drink and spit out nasty comments at me.

I lean my head against Ten's back and marvel how different hugging him feels from hugging Alexander. The difference comes from all the thoughts in my head and the feelings I have for those two. I think I love them both but there's only one of them I'm very likely in love with. I'm curious to meet Ten's plus one, the necessarily handsome Italian model who is making my best friend so happy.

We reach the Clark's estate and sure enough, Alexander is waiting for us. First I only see his ride and then, when I see him, the smile on my face goes from ear to ear. The thought of hiding how happy I am to see him does not even cross my mind. My heart is soaring and when I get into his arms I truly feel at home.

"I've missed you, Love," he says. "I thought this week would never end."

I never get a chance to answer as he leans over and kisses me. Ten walks away from us and says, "I'll be in the house when you too are done. This is getting way to mushy for me!"

I feel Alexander's lips curl up in a smile but he does not stop what he's doing and I'm relishing the sensations. I wish there was a way to store it somewhere so I could replay it at will. But then again if there were such a thing it would lose it's magic! He lets me go with a peck on the nose. I'm in a pink little cloud.

Alexander takes his saddlebag from the bike and we walk in the house by the kitchen door that Ten has left slightly ajar for us. The house is nice and warm and we remove our coats as we walk through the kitchen into the gigantic main room. It's a dining room, living room, family room all in one. In one corner of the room there's Carla's baby grand piano and next to it, James Senior's desk. Ten told me his grandfather loves to work to the sound of his daughter's music.

Alexander sees the piano and cannot resist its call. It's a beautiful Steinway. I don't know much about musical instruments but I'm sure whatever James purchased for his daughter is certainly top of the line.

Alexander drops his bag by the piano and moves the stool to adjust the distance to the length of his legs as he lifts the keyboard cover. He places his hands on the keys and starts to play with his eyes closed. It's a slow ballad. The rhythm changes several times during the piece, it's romantic and just a little bit sad. I stand by his side, my hands on the black lacquer top, the vibrations invading my body through the tips of my fingers.

When he finishes playing he looks at me. There's a question in his look. "I love it. It's breathtaking," I say. "Did you write this?" He nods and offers one of hands to pull me to him. "You need lyrics for it," I tell him.

"Yes I do. We have the weekend to work on it."

"We?" I ask, raising my eyebrows. "I've never written anything."

"So you're a poem virgin too," he says gently mocking me. "Seriously, you're the only girl I know who has not even dabbled in this."

I close my eyes and realize that no matter what I'm doing, I can't escape the Bitch's influence. I've never allowed myself to think about putting feelings to paper. How could I when my privacy can be violated at any time? Furthermore I'm pretty sure that if I had been brave enough to try, she would have found it and then humiliated me by making fun of whatever I had come up with. I've denied myself for so long that I'm not even sure I ever wanted to write stuff anyway.

Alexander does not stop to consider that I could possibly not want to do this with him. "We'll do this together," he says taking a notebook from his bag, there's a pen attached to the cover. He flips it open and looks for a blank page. He scoots over on the stool and invites me to sit next to him. When I do, he hands me the notebook and says, "I'll start from the top and hum so you can get a feel for the melody."

"Did you decide what the lyrics are going to be about?" Ten asks. He's magically appeared behind us. Actually, he probably came in while Alexander was playing and I was so wrapped up in the melody I didn't notice.

"Yes, I think it should be about missing the person you long to be with," Alexander says looking at me intently.

"That works for me," I tell him.

"Okay guys, I'll let you write. I actually have some studying to do so I'll go up in my old room. If you're done before me, come and get me."

"Will do," I say as Ten leaves the room.

Alexander starts to play and hums the melody. He looks at me and says, "Come on. You start. Give me something to begin with."

"I never would have guessed how much I'd miss you," I say.

He smiles and says, "I like that." He starts again and sings, "I never would have guessed how much I'd miss you; How could I when I barely know you. How did I let you in so fast? What do we do to make it last?" He hums and looks at me expectantly, "Your turn, Love."

Two hours later we have a cute love song. It's not great poetry. A far cry from the English sonnets they make us study in school but it works for a song. It's simple enough that you can memorize the lyrics after hearing the song a couple of times. The melody is catchy.

Just on cue Ten comes down from his room and asks to hear our masterpiece. I joke that he may be overconfident in our talents as writers. Actually I think what we did is pretty lame but then most love songs are if you look at them with a critical eye. I scold myself. This is Ten, he's my friend, he won't have a critical eye. He'll be supportive.

We agree to try it out on him and Alexander starts to sing. Ten raises his hand to stop him. "I'll be right back." He runs up to his room and comes back with a square box he sets on the piano. "It's cassette payer and recorder," he explains, "Of course the sound will not be great but I will hold the first recording of this hit song!"

Ten presses on two of the device's keys as Alexander begins to sing again and Ten stops him after on sentence.

"What now?"

"Why isn't Lovey singing it with you?"

Alexander turns around and asks, "You can sing?"

"I can carry a tune," I say, "but nothing that compares to your amazing voice."

"Let me be the judge of that. Please, sing with me, Love."

He starts again and I join him. Our voices work well together. I keep my eyes on the notebook to make sure that I get it right and when we're done, Alexander looks at me as if he's seeing me for the first time. I'm embarrassed because I don't know what he's thinking. Ten gives us a standing ovation.

"You can sing," Alexander says, and now that I know that he likes my voice, I think I'm glowing.

"I'm honored to be the witness of this new partnership," Ten says with a mock grandiose tone of voice. "You guys were made to make beautiful music together." I giggle. I don't think I used to giggle that much before. This is fun. No matter how long it lasts, I will enjoy every minute of it.

Ten continues to gloat and says, "I told you she could sing." He's grinning like mad. Sometimes the mischievous 12 years old he must have been pops up to the surface. He's cute but very annoying. "You've got to know she would have had the lead in all her high school musicals if her mother ..."

"Ten, please," I interrupt him.

"No, let him speak, I want to know." Alexander says, "Why wouldn't she let you do it? Wouldn't it make her look good in front of her friends?"

I look at my hands and force myself to put them flat on my thighs. Alexander looks at me strangely, like he can't comprehend that a mother would hate her daughter so much. I know few people get it but that's the way it is and I can't do anything about it. Every so often I ask myself why she does hate me so much. I think maybe something horrible happened to her to make her that way but I don't let my mind go there. I just hate her, it's easier that way.

"Can we please not talk about her," I ask.

"Sure, Lovey" Ten says, "I'm sorry I did."

"Well I'm not sorry he made you show me how good your voice is," Alexander says, pushing my curtain of hair away from my face. Let's sing it again one more time to make sure we're happy with it."

Chapter 6

I'm standing outside waiting for my ride. The place will be closed tonight. No one wants to celebrate the end of the year in a diner. Tomorrow morning will be another story. It's one very busy morning. It will be almost as busy as a summer holiday weekend. I'm happy that I don't have to work then. No matter how good the tips would be they would not be good enough for putting up with the Bitch at her worst. She'll probably show up with a monster hangover. Wendy will have to deal with her. She has barely spoken to me since Saturday and I'm ashamed I have not asked her how she's doing.

I'll ask when I'll get back to work after school next week. Right now, I'm in my little bubble of bliss and I'm not letting any misery in. The bubble has a short expiration date. Too soon it will burst as Alexander rides away.

I don't know how I will hold myself together since Ten will also be gone all the way to Europe for one term but I'm sure I'll find a way. It's not as if I had a choice. I've gotta keep this up for a few more months, just until I finish high school and then I'll be able to run away. My plan is to work for a year, settle down and then start college.

Alexander is the one who picks me up today. He's been enjoying this long weekend in the Clark's house. He's fallen in love with the piano and says that when he has enough money he will purchase one just like that. I know most girls my age would wonder how long it takes before one gets accepted as a star and invited by other stars to cool parties and fancy television shows. That's not the questions that come to my mind. Mine are not so glittery. I'm a boring down to earth girl. What I really want to know is how long does it take for a rock star to make enough money to buy a Steinway? I have no idea how much a tour brings in. Or maybe it does not bring in anything but helps you sell records and establish yourself as an artist? Then the income would be from the sales? I want to ask Alexander but I don't because I fear my curiosity about the music industry will make me look like I'm a money greedy girlfriend.

I smile as he gets closer. What I truly am is a time greedy girlfriend. I want every second he can give to me before he goes on the road. I realize this may be all the time I'll ever get with him. He's going to be a star and I'll probably lose him when it happens but, at least he'll have been mine for a little while.

He stops just long enough for me to hop on behind him and strap my helmet on. We ride away and I don't even look to see if the Bitch is watching me go. We reach the Clark's estate and Alexander drives straight to the main house. Ten's bike is nowhere to be seen.

"He's gone back to the city," Alexander tells me. "There's some big parties he wanted to attend and he thought that we didn't really need him."

"Oh, okay," is all I manage to say. I've got mixed feelings about this. On one hand, I'm kinda happy he's gone because ... well there's stuff, cuddling stuff, Alexander and I can't do when Ten's around but then, on the other hand, I'm a little sad too. I like having my buddy around and I was eager to meet the person that put that dreamy smile on his face.

"Before he left, he showed me how the hot tub works, I really liked it in there the other night. I thought we should do it again but just the two of us."

"I really liked it too," I say. "I had never been in the tub during the colder months. It's delicious to stay neck deep in scalding water while it's cold out."

"Yes it's very decadent to watch the steam come up and be so warm. That may be another thing on my purchase list when I've finally made it."

"Let me guess. Will the first thing you'll get be a grand piano?"

"No, first I need to get the home in which to put the piano. The first thing I'll do when I'll have money is to buy a roof to go over my head," he says. He grins and adds "Then I'll get a bed and then a piano and possibly a hot tub."

There was another perk to out bathing the other night, I got a better look at Alexander's body. He's a bit more squarely built than Ten but they have a similar swimmer's body. I know Ten trains with his university swimming team. I have no clue how Alexander keeps such an amazing shape.

It was cute to see Alexander in one of Ten's bathing suits that evening. Bathing suit ... I didn't bring one this time. Before I even think about it, I protest, "We can't, I don't have a suit."

He looks at me as if my answer is the most ridiculous thing he's ever heard. I'm pretty sure I'm turning crimson red because my cheeks feel really very warm right now. Okay, I can do without a bathing suit. I'm trying to remember what underwear I have put on this morning and realize that the stuff I'm wearing is so old and washed out that I will feel less self conscious without anything than in my undies. How weird am I?

"I won't be wearing anything either," he says with a grin. "Come on, let's get this show on the road."

After dropping that bomb in my mind he takes my hand and start walking towards the house. Am I ready for this? I'm not sure anymore. We walk into the big house and drop our stuff in the main room that overlooks the deck where the hottub is located. I look around the room and think that it's not in too bad a shape for a place in which two guys have been left to their own devices with no one to remind them they need to clean up.

He removes his jacket and kicks his boots off before he hops on the couch and holds his arms out to me. I do the same and cuddle on the couch next to him. He massages my shoulders and I purr. "Ahhh, this is heaven."

"My Mum used to give me great back rubs," he says. "She would go on for hours. Andy and I were very spoiled that way."

"Andy is your elder brother?" I ask.

"Yes. I told you he's a cop in the city. He's always wanted to be a police officer. Mum and I used to call him officer Andrew when we wanted to tease him. Officer Andrew's favorite thing is foot massages. That's what he loved best so that's what she did for him."

I know his mom's gone and that he was raised by an uncle. He's the man who owns the bar he works in. He never mentions a father. I would like to know more about his mom and his family but I'm not brave enough to ask because I can see that it's bittersweet for him to talk about her.

"What about you?" he asks. "Surely you have some positive memories with your mother, no?"

"No. None at all." My tone is clipped, almost aggressive. I can see from the look in his eyes that he's not going to let it go. Very few persons know how evil and cruel she truly is behind the respectable façade she puts on for the world. I want to let it go and talk about something else but he seems to want to get to the bottom of this.

I think about it and stand up straighter pulling away from him. The magic is gone. I guess it will not come back unless I make him see that she's something I don't even want to talk about. The power she has over my life even when she's not there unsettles me. "You really want to know?"

"I want to know everything about you."

I close my eyes because I don't want to see a look of pity on his face as I begin to tell him one of my most telling horror stories. "When I was ten, on my way back from school I found a kitten in the street. I could not resist the little ball of fur."

"Right, nothing's cuter than a kitten," he says.

"So I picked her up and brought her home. For two days I kept it in my room, I sneaked up some food from the kitchen, made a kitty litter with a shoe box and sand I brought from the beach..." I take a deep breath and continue. "On the third day, when I got home from school, the Bitch was in my room, sitting on my bed with the kitten on her lap. The little baby was purring away." My voice is shaking but now I need to get the rest of the story out. I give him a short version. "She drowned it in the kitchen sink. She had waited for me to get home to do it because she made me watch."

There's a look of disbelief on his face and he's about to say something so I put two fingers on his lips to silence him.

"I cried for days and the Bitch patiently waited for me to stop crying before going for her second kill. That's when she told me that it was all my fault. If I had left the lost kitten on the side of the street, it would still be alive. It could have found its mother and be kept safe, it could have been adopted by someone else walking down the road and brought to a cat loving family ... If the kitten was dead it was because I had not listened to her. I had brought a pet home while I knew she did not want a pet.

So the kitten's death was on me." I shudder and look into Alexander's eyes and I see compassion. My fingers are still on his mouth he kisses them and then pulls me back in his arms.

He holds me tight and says, "Don't you see it's a load of bull? You're not really responsible. I mean, there were so many other things she could have done. She could have looked for another family for the kitten. If she did not want to be bothered, she could have brought it to the ASPCA shelter in the next town. She could even have made you take it to the pound or she could even have tossed it out back on the street. She didn't have to kill it, make you watch, and then make you feel guilty. That's on her, not on you."

Alexander is rocking me gently and his tender gesture doesn't open a floodgate. I will not cry again over the kitten or over the tortured child that I was. "Maybe," I say. "Maybe you're right but you know, I still feel it's my fault and I'm responsible."

"I'm sorry, Love. Now let's get you in a more cheerful mood," he says. "Do you want to eat now or should be try the hot bubbles?"

"I'm not really hungry yet." The answer has come spontaneously out of my mouth before I took anytime to think and as he says, "Hot tub it is then." I realize I'm going to have to undress and I feel very self-conscious. It's not only that I'm going to be without clothes but also the fact that, without Ten around, if one of the Clark's family member was to drop in unexpectedly it would look like we're trespassing.

As if reading my mind, again, Alexander says, "Before he left Ten spoke to his grandfather in Acapulco and checked with his parents. We really have the house to ourselves tonight. Ten's locked the bungalow so I'll sleep in his old room. Do you know that his room is larger than my entire studio in the city? I could get used to living like this."

"Well give it a few months and you'll be able to, Mister Super Star," I say while he's fumbling with his belt. I gather all my courage and quickly unhook my bra under my T-shirt so I will be able to remove both at the same time. I open my jeans and get ready to push them down with my panties.

I raise my eyes to him before doing it and see that he's already naked. My eyes remain on his face. He smiles at me and says, "I'll go get towels now so we don't freeze when we get out."

As he walks toward the bathroom I tear my clothes away and let everything drop to the floor. I rush to open the sliding doors and step on the deck. Wow, it's a lot colder out here. I have goose pimples all over. In two seconds the tip of my breasts have turned into red skittles. I push the hot tub cover away and step down in the water. It is scalding hot. I fumble with the command buttons on the side and find the timer for the bubbles. Within seconds the mechanism starts and the surface of the water is covered with bubbles and foam. It's silly, but now that the water is no longer transparent I don't feel as naked.

Alexander arrives a couple of minutes later with large towels that he drops on the deck by the steps. He's scrumptious to look at. He jumps in next to me and moans like it's the most delicious thing ever. He's a warm water guy. He sits down across from me. There's a little ledge that serves as a bench and runs around the tub at half height. He looks at me without saying anything and then moves over to the center of the tub. He kneels in front of me putting his arms around my waist.

This is perfect. I think I could stay like this forever.

"I'll show you something even better," he says. Did I speak out loud again? He shifts position at the bottom of the tub and pulls me on his lap.

I snuggle against him as he's caressing my hair and then he raises my head with a knuckle under my chin and slants his mouth over mine. I open my lips and melt. Again. He's got this magic power to turn me into some sort of liquid state. My head spins. I feel dizzy and I lean into him.

He threads his fingers in my hair and pulls his lips away from mine for an instant to tell me, "If you'll let me I will keep you safe. It would make me feel ten feet tall if you would let me take care of you."

Chapter 7

I love that he wants to take care of me. I want to believe that he means what he says. I know better however. For now, it's nothing more than a dream. He's going on tour next week and I'm going back to my sucky life of school and diner's shifts.

"You don't believe me, Love, do you?" Alexander asks.

"I know you mean it," I tell him "but there's the logistics of life."

"What do you mean?"

"I'm eighteen. You're what? Twenty and change?"

He nods and smiles when I say, "Technically I just stopped qualifying as jailbait." I run my fingers in his hair. "I want to finish school and you want to go on tour. You'll have to wait until I'm done here to become my knight in shinning armor. For now, you have swept me of my feet but you're not going to carry me away into the sunset."

"You're right, it's not going to be this sunset but give me a little credit, I will not vanish. I'm yours to keep."

I'm about to kiss him when he adds, "So I've swept you of your feet," with a delicious grin.

"What do you think?" I snap going in full sarcasm mode, "I'm sitting on your lap naked and kissing you like there's no tomorrow."

He kisses me again and his hands slide from the top of my shoulders to the small of my back and then further down to my buttock. His hands come back up and cup my breasts and I'm swimming in lust. There's a need inside me that I have never felt before and it's eating me alive. I hold on to him for balance with my hands on his shoulders.

"You wanna know what I think? I think that I want you so bad that if you'll let me I will make love to you all through the New Year. Will you let me?"

My eyes riveted in his, I nod.

"Say it," Alexander growls. "Tell me you want me. I need to hear you say it. I need to be sure this is what you want because if I start there will be no going back, you'll be mine for good."

"Yes, this is what I want," I whisper, "I want you to be my first. I want you to show me, I need more of you." Alexander lifts me from his lap and gently moves us until we're kneeling face to face. His upper torso is out of the water but he seems oblivious to the cold.

"No one, no one ever before," he says. It's not a question. It's an affirmation. It's like he needs to say it aloud, like it's the most amazing thing that ever happened to him. He'll be the first. He's looking at me as if I'm the most attractive girl on earth and for an instant I think that maybe I am. For sure I'm the luckiest. A lusty creature has taken over in my head. She's locked all negative thoughts in a closet in the back of my mind and I can barely hear them banging against the door.

Time is standing still as we look into each other's eyes drinking up each other's soul. I repeat after him "No one, no one ever before ... and I wish for no one, no one ever after."

That undoes him. His hands move from my waist to my back and he pulls me closer. I can feel his need is matching mine and, when he kisses me again, I close my eyes to savor the sensation and can't help but moan in his mouth. He slides a hand to the apex of my legs and as he explores the fold, my eyes fly open in wonder at the sensation. He pulls back a little and studies the expression on my face looking for clues to adapt his caress to my needs. His touch has created a ball of fire that is overtaking me.

"Can you tell me what you feel?" he asks.

I'm panting. The sensation is so new and so incredible, I'm at a loss for words. I tell him the first image that comes to my mind. "I'm standing on the edge of a cliff, I have this irresistible urge to jump but I don't know how."

"I'll show you, Love," he says. And he does.

I let him push me over the edge and instead of free falling, I fly. I fly away so high I never want it to stop. When it does stop, Alexander is there to catch me and he cradles me in his arm until I catch my breath and then he starts again but this time it's not his hands that enter me.

He goes very slowly to give me time to adjust. His eyes are closed and his face is a mask of concentration. Every time he gets a little deeper my breath catches. I know he's fully in me when he raises his open his eyes and looks at me. "How do you feel?" he asks.

"I'm fine," I say. I'm not sure if I really am. I feel very stretched and it's strange.

"Fine's not good enough," he says as he pulls out slowly and then back in again. I shudder and he asks, "better?"

I nod. I'm not sure I can speak right now. He smiles and quickens the pace. I close my eyes and I surrender totally to him. He's a part of me now and we merge in the most marvelous sunburst.

He holds me without moving while we both catch our breath and then he slowly pulls out and gets out of the water. He wraps himself in a towel and opens another one for me to snuggle into as I get out. He pulls the winter cover over the hot tub and we both run back in the house and into what used to be Ten's room before he moved to the bungalow. We dive under the thick quilt of his tiny bed and warm up in each other's arms.

"How do you feel?" Alexander asks again.

"Happy, a little bit sore and worried."

"Why worried?"

"Because we did not use any protection," I say.

Alexander laughs. "Yes, I thought about it but I did not see how I was going to put a condom in the tub. Also, I think the water was too hot for any of my swimmers to survive, so you shouldn't worry, we're good."

"You're sure?"

"Positive and when we do it again, I have condoms. You need to trust me a bit, Love. My intentions are not pure, obviously, but they're really good. I promise, I won't do to you anything you don't want me to do."

"Hmmm hmmm," I say, "I'm going to close my eyes for a minute." I roll over and in Ten's boyhood bed, we sleep and fit together like spoons in a drawer.

I wake up to the sound of Alexander softly snoring in my ear. His head is in the clouds. He's fast asleep. Another part of his anatomy is wide awake. There's a clock ticking on the nightstand. It's an old round model with Mickey Mouse's ears. It's five to twelve. Incongruous, next to this childhood icon there's a handful of condoms.

Alexander came prepared but obviously he had not counted on the impractical aspect of the hot tub. I hope he's right about the effect of the scalding waters on sperm.

I'm starving for food and for Alexander's attention. Not necessarily in that order. I think I know how I want to put the year 1978 to rest.

I take a condom and turn around to face Alexander. I tear the foil and study it's content. It's like a sock that would have been rolled down a leg. To put it on one needs to roll it up. Okay, I can do that ... I lift the quilt and after a little fumbling, I roll the thin membrane slowly down his length. Alexander's hips move in my direction and when I look up to his face I see he's no longer asleep. His eyes are wide open and he's grinning.

"I love a woman who takes the initiative," he says as he rolls on his back taking me with him. "I can't think of a more glorious way to celebrate the New Year."

Neither can I. I straddle him and lower myself on his length, slowly. We move together. It's a sensual ballet. I have this image of a tango dance. Except tango is black and white and now I see a million colors, and fireworks and endless bliss. Making love is magical. I don't think I'll ever tire of this.

"Well I sure hope not!" Alexander says.

Hear, hear, I've done it again. Spoken my thought out loud.

I try not to think about what's going to happen with us. Maybe it's better that we don't see the future. If it's not good we'll know it soon enough. If it's good, we'll enjoy it even more by being surprised.

SECOND PART
- 1979 À 1980 -

Chapter 8

It's the middle of the night and there's this horrible pain in my back. It's as if someone is stabbing me repeatedly with an icepick. Maybe it's a stomach virus. Something I ate for dinner does not agree with me. I go back to sleep.

It comes back with a vengeance. I open my eyes and go into full denial mode. It's too early. It's not been a full nine months yet. But the truth is that I'm not really sure what the date is. I've lost track of time. I close my eyes and breathe deeply. I doze again.

When the third wave of pain subsides, I sit up in my bed and get dressed. I hate those-tent like dresses I have been wearing lately.

Once I'm dressed I go back to bed praying it's a false alarm and fall asleep again.

I grit my teeth. What is giving birth going to be like if this is *just* what the labor pains feel like? The thought sets me in a panic and I pound on the door of my room hoping that I'm going to be loud enough to wake my two jailers.

I've been having frightful dreams about delivering the baby by myself, all alone in my room. I pound on the door again and listen for any noise that would indicate that they've heard me. I yell, "Maria, Maria, can you hear me? The baby's coming."

I'm about to kick the door when the contractions return. I take two steps back and curl up on the bed. I twist around looking for a comfortable position. My efforts are in vain. I guess there are no such positions when you're in labor. I try the short breathing I've seen people do in movies but it does not do a thing for me.

The door opens and Miguel looks at me and says, "Stop screaming. You're scaring Maria."

I had not realized I was screaming but I must have been because my throat hurts. Maria pushes him aside and comes kneel by my bed. She's dressed. She touches my belly. I'm as tense as a drum. She turns around and says to her husband, "Go get the car, the baby's coming now."

Miguel turns around and leaves. I look in Maria's eyes. I know she's a good person, I think she likes me so I plead with her, "Maria, please, I beg of you, let me go or take me to the hospital." If she takes me to the private institution where I've been getting my checkups, I know they will take the baby away from me and that will be the end of me. I can't let that happen.

Maria brushes my hair from my forehead and hushes me. "It's gonna be all right, Lyv," she says. "It's for the best, little girl. I know you don't want to hear that now but you're barely eighteen. What would you do with a baby when you're still a baby yourself?"

I can't agree with her but at least she's caring. She truly thinks that abandoning my child will be to my benefit. But that's not why it's happening. That's not the way the Bitch sees it. She was the first to realize I was pregnant. What tipped her of was the fact that I didn't get my monthly migraine for two months. When a third month passed, she knew. By then I had become aware of the situation too.

"Your coming into this world was a mistake. It was my mistake so I had no choice but to pay the price," the Bitch said and then pointing to my belly, she hissed between clenched teeth, "This one is your mistake and I will not be responsible for what's to become of it."

"That's fine," I had told her. "I will move out at the end of the school year and you will not have to take care of me anymore."

I didn't really have a plan but I still had several months to figure it out. Ten was coming back from Europe for Spring break and he would help me find a solution. I didn't care if Alexander wanted the baby or not, of course I wished he would, but in any case that baby was my responsibility and I was going to be as good a mother as mine had been dreadful.

Life went back to normal for a couple of weeks and then, one evening, she had me kidnapped. Two men came for me a little after school. They drugged me and carried me out on a gurney to an ambulance. I phased in and out for a full day and woke up in this windowless room. How many days have gone by since? I don't know. I lost count.

What I know for a fact, on the other hand, is that the Bitch has come up with a convincing story to tell everyone at home. She's so attached to appearances I have no doubt her lie is good and everyone's bought her story. She likes being seen as a victim so she's probably acting distraught and telling every one how worried she is that I ran away. Who knows? It should be around the end of the summer, it's still hot and it's very humid. When I get a look at the outside world it seems to be raining all the time.

During the first weeks I made Maria's life hell. Every single time she opened the door, I fought her and tried to escape. Every single time Miguel was right behind me and dragged me back in my room kicking and screaming. I swear the man will never forget me. He now has scars on his face and on his arms to remember me by. I gave it all I had.

God, did I fight. I stopped when the struggles brought about contractions. Maria warned me: "If you keep that up you're going to lose the baby."

Well now it's happening. I'm about to lose my baby. I feel so helpless. I hate it. I need to find a way out of here. I know where we're going. We've been at the medical center eight times already to get me checked up and supervised. The first time they gave me all kinds of blood tests and then they pronounced me healthy as a horse and free from any diseases. They prescribed a diet that Maria has made me follow religiously. I don't think any one had ever taken such good care of me before but I can't enjoy it because it's all for the wrong reason.

They are not taking care of me for me, they are treating me like a giant incubator. For them I'm this baby manufacturing machine they need to maintain to get a perfect product in the end. On the way to the center for checkups, I was able to figure out that that the facility where I am to give birth is located near a town called Jupiter. The facility is run by some cult and it's organized like a high security prison. Once Maria and her husband check me in I'll never be able to escape. I've been there enough to realize that.

Every single time I was there, Maria and Miguel made sure that I never met anybody else but the staff. Nevertheless I got a glimpse of several pregnant girls and once in a while I heard babies cry. My guess is that it's the maternity ward of a home for pregnant girls.

As the pain recedes, Maria helps me get in a sitting position and gently gets me up on my feet and down the stairs of the house. She makes me sit in front of a large fan and explains that we're going to wait a little while. Miguel's gone to get the car. The fresh air from the fan is a welcome treat. I fall asleep almost right away. Not for long.

A few contraction sets later, Maria wakes me up and says, "Come on, Lyv. You need to walk out to the car before the next contraction comes."

I follow her. This trip is my last chance to escape but I'm big and so tired, I can barely walk by myself. Maria sits in the back of the car with me. She lays me down with my head on her knees and cradles me in her arms. "It's going to be all right," she says. "The doctors are going to give you something for the pain. Come on baby, just a little while longer and it will be fine. Take a deep breath."

I don't want to breathe. I want to die. But then if I die now I will kill my baby. What kind of mother would that make me? The pain comes back and I scream. It's not only the pain, it's the frustration, the helplessness. I'm hurt and angry. I kick the door of the car every time the contractions come back. Miguel curses under his breath in Spanish and Maria scolds him. As if I cared about what he's saying. I'm in so much pain, I don't care about anything else.

We reach our destination and Miguel jumps out to open the door on my side. Maria gently tries to push me out of the car. I refuse to move. I know I'm not making sense but I won't budge. As long as I'm in the car I'm not having my baby and as long as I'm not having my baby, they can't take him or her away from me.

Miguel understands they won't be able to handle me alone. He goes to get help. This is my last chance. If I make it to the main road maybe a car will stop and help me escape. I muster all my strength and manage to slide out of the car. I lean on the side of the vehicle to get on my feet. I start to walk back in the direction we just came from before Maria understands what's happening.

I'm just a few feet away from the car when the next contraction hits. Hell, it's getting worse. I can't breathe. I grit my teeth and take one more step. *Come on, Lyv, you can do it.* Just one more step. My legs fail me and I fall to my hands and knees on the gravel. The combined pains are excruciating. I breathe in and scream, "Help, somebody help me please!"

On all fours now I try to move further away from the car. I can barely budge and then strong hands pick me up. I'm lifted on a gurney.

This is it. I lost. The Bitch wins.

I'm going to lose my baby.

They wheel me into a delivery room. The contractions are closer and closer as well as stronger and stronger. Time has taken a strange turn. It stretches forever during the contractions and then flies away in between. I've totally lost all sense of time. I don't know if it's been hours or days. This can't go on for much longer. If it does I'll die of exhaustion.

The midwife looks tired too and Maria seems worried. She coos at me and wipes my forehead with a towel. Maria's been next to me the entire time holding my hand. It's so perverse that the only comfort I'm getting now is provided by the woman who's dragged me here.

"Almost done," says the midwife.

I'm so tired I don't even have the strength to follow her instructions. When she says push, I try to push but it doesn't seem to do anything. I scream in pain and frustration. A soft woman's voice asks if they can't give me something for the pain and the midwife answers "In pain you shall bring forth children."

No kidding!

After what seems like an eternity, the midwife says, "One more and we'll be done." I try to push again, I give it all I have and I hear a baby wail. The midwife clamps the umbilical cord and wraps the baby in a small cloth. "It's a girl," she says.

A woman I had not seen before steps in my line of vision. She's in her twenties and very pretty. She takes my daughter in her arms. She looks lovingly at her and says, "Hello, welcome to the world, little Eve."

Her voice is very melodious and there's a lilt to her speech, probably a southern accent. I can't identify it precisely. She's the one who asked if there was nothing to help me with the pain. I look at her and start to sob uncontrollably. This woman is going to take my baby away and there is nothing I can do about it. I'm too weak to fight and even if I did find it in me to stand, they would overpower me in a second.

The woman turns around to looks at me and she tells me, "I'm going to take very good care of her, I promise. I've been waiting for her for so long, she's going to be the happiest little girl on the planet." I can see she means it but it doesn't make it hurt less.

The midwife presses on my tummy and looks a little worried. "Got to get the placenta out," she says to Maria who's still holding my hand. It's so weird the way she won't look at me when she says that.

"I'm sorry dear," she says, "but I have no choice but to do this." I'm not sure who she's talking too but she takes my daughter back from the woman's arms and brings her to me. "Right now this little girl needs to get some food."

She sits me up and tells me there's nothing better for a baby that her mother's milk. I'm overjoyed. Maybe I'll get to spend some time with my little girl. Maybe I'll get another chance to run with her but then the midwife pulls away the sheet that covers me and while she puts my baby in my arms and one of my nipples in her mouth she tells me breast feeding is going to do me good.

"Breast feeding causes contractions that help the uterus expel the placenta. So don't be startled if you feel new contractions. It's part of a normal process," she explains to me and I understand that this is the reason why I get to hold my daughter, the placenta's not coming out spontaneously. My daughter starts nursing and indeed, it feels as if there's a direct line between my breasts and my lower regions. The new contractions are not nearly as painful as before. They're mild enough that I can think about something else.

I can think about Eve.

If I can't find a way to escape with her, her name is going to be Eve. Actually it could be her name no matter what. It's pretty, I like it.

Her beautiful grey eyes lock onto mine and I dissolve in a torrent of tears. Eve frowns, I don't think it's my tears, it's the concentration. Nursing looks like hard work. After a few minutes she stops and falls asleep the nipple still in her mouth while the contractions continue. The midwife looks happy. The placenta is coming out.

Chapter 9

Now I know, it's in Florida that I've been locked up.

The train ride back to New York takes forever. I look through the window but I don't really see anything. I feel numb. I stopped feeling when they took Eve away after two days of nursing.

I know it's my own fault if I only had her for two days and not a week as they had originally planned but I have no regrets. I had to try to get away at least one more time. I'm glad I did.

Obviously trying to set the building on fire was not such a clever idea but that was the only thing that I could think of that would force them to throw all the doors wide open. I look at the picnic bag Maria gave me as she sat me in the train. There's a bottle of water and a couple of sandwiches. I'm parched. Lately I've always felt parched. I've turned into a milk manufacturing plant, I guess I need fluids.

Well except there's no one to manufacture the milk for anymore. One of the nurses or rather wardens told me to look for milk banks. I had no idea there was such a thing but it seems they've been around since the beginning of the century. I understand that women with too much milk can go "pump-up" in those places and give away their production.

One of the other girls in the ward advised me against it. She said pumping keeps the machine going and I probably don't want to do that. She's right, I don't. But still, I'm parched so I drink the water and stare outside again.

Eve's adoptive mother looked like a caring woman. She was very sweet to me. She told me Eve would see a lot of the world. Her husband shushed her. I guess he wanted me to know as little about them as possible. It was a bit silly, when they spoke in front of me, he called her "wife" instead of using her first name. I had never heard someone talk to a spouse that way. He seems very devoted to her but not really a baby guy. "Wife" will have to make sure that Eve grows on him.

All things considered her life will very likely be easier with them than it would have been with me. Before they left, I asked her, "Will you tell her she's adopted?" The woman said no. Maybe it's better this way. I'm not sure I would have had an appropriate message for this woman to give her from me. I just pray that she'll be happy.

I fall asleep. When I wake up my picnic bag is gone. Well, I wasn't going to eat it anyway. I still have my own bag I was using as a pillow. I do the inventory. Two jeans, three tee-shirts and some underwear. I'm still wearing one of my tents. Everything in this bag is probably too small. I know the bras are for sure.

At the bottom of the bag there's some small change. In the bag pocket there's a train ticket to go from New York City to Long Island. As if I were ever going back there! I shred the ticket in tiny pieces and as I drop the confetti in the ashtray, I realize I could probably have obtained a refund. That was dumb. I hit my head against the window. Why am I so stupid?

I need to find a job. I need to get a life.

I go back to sleep and wake up in Manhattan. I exit the train and the station. At the corner of the street there are four phones. Two are out of order and only one of the two others is busy. I take a dime of my pocket and dial Ten's number. I silently pray for him to answer but on the fourth ring the answering machine picks up. I hate talking to machines. I'm about to hang up and then think better of it. The least I can do is leave a message to let him know I'm all right.

The machine beeps and I start to talk, "Ten, it's me..." and then I stop because I don't know what more to say. What could I possibly tell him, that I'm fine? I'm not. Well not really. "I just wanted to speak with you," I say and then I hear a click and Ten's voice.

"Lovey, is that you?"

Listening to the sound of his voice and his name for me is so good. It's overwhelming. I laugh and cry at the same time and barely manage to say, "Yes."

"Where are you Lovey?" he asks. His voice is choked.

"Penn station," I say. "Across from the post office."

"Okay. Don't move. Stay there. I'm coming for you. I'll be with you in twenty minutes."

I hang up the phone and start pacing. I've spent so much time locked up in my room and unable to see my feet that just being able to walk freely and to look at my toes feels exhilarating. I need to concentrate on the little joys to forget the bigger pain. I eavesdrop on the conversation of the woman who's still speaking on the corner phone. She's telling a friend about a blind date from hell. She's funny and listening to her description of the sorry ass she spent the evening with gets a smile on my face.

"So finally he said, 'I'm not a breast man, I'm more into butts than breasts,'" she tells her friend. "Can you imagine the nerve of this guy? So I just got up and walked away ... yeah, you're right, that gave him a chance to appreciate my butt and to find out what he missed for arriving late." She laughs and swears that she'll never again go on a blind date.

I don't know if it's her good humor or the pulse of the city or yet again the fact that Ten is coming to get me but I'm starting to feel better. I look around. Just from where I'm standing I can see a dozen restaurants. I won't have a problem finding a job in this city. I just need to whip myself into shape and buy some new clothes. To do that I need to get my money out of my saving accounts. I left my saving pass with Martha. I'm pretty sure it remained safe with her and she'll mail it to me when I ask her.

I'm still pacing when Ten arrives. He's carrying an extra helmet strapped around his elbow. I run to him and hug him fiercely, "Please take me away from here."

He blinks and gives me the second helmet. I grab it and hop in behind him. At least the tent like dress I'm wearing is wide enough to keep me decent while we ride. I'm sore and the vibrations of the machine are painful on my lower regions but I don't care. I'm free. Another twenty minutes through rush hour traffic and we descend in the parking garage of his building. We dismount and he takes my bag and my hand as we walk to the elevators. He's holding my hand so tight it's almost too much but I'm fine with it. I so badly need the connection.

The garage is busy. People are coming and going. A couple of mechanics are working on a car. Just as we walk in the elevator, another couple arrives. They're on their way to the penthouse. We stop two floors before. We enter his apartment and Ten calls out as he walks me through the living room, "Anybody home?"

No one answers. I guess we're alone. We enter Ten's bedroom suite and he slams the door behind us, drops our stuff on his desks and takes my face in his hands. He looks at me intently as if trying to make sure I'm all right. I can see that he's relieved to have me here but still concerned.

"Your mother said you ran away. I didn't believe her for a second. If you had run you would have run to me or to Xander, not away from us." I nod. I love that he never doubted me. I adore that he did not believe her. I know his trust and his love for me are as unconditional as mine for him.

"What happened?" he asks. "Where have you been? I've been worried sick about you." I want to tell him everything but I don't know where to start. I wrap my arms around him and rest my head on his chest. His hand is messing up my hair. "Come on, Lovey, talk to me."

"I was in Florida, locked up for months." I say and my voice turns into a whisper as I tell him, "I just had a baby. A little girl and they took her away from me."

He holds me tight as I tell him about the windowless room and Maria and Miguel. I tell him about Eve and how I failed her and how I failed Alexander and myself. I tell him I'm never going back to the Bitch's place.

When I'm done speaking, he just says, "Right now you need to rest. You're going to stay with me at least until you get your strength back and then you'll see what you want to do." His voice is so cold, it scares me.

"Are you mad?" I ask him.

He lifts my head to look into my eyes, "Mad as hell but not at you, Baby, never at you." There's something different about him. It's not just the fact that he called me baby, which he's never done before, it's something else and I can't put my finger on it.

He looks around in his drawers for one large tee shirt and then walks with me to the adjacent bathroom. He has a gigantic shower. A nice change from the tiny cubicle I had to use lately at the clinic. "Come on Lovey, get ready for bed. I know it's early but you look like you need to get some sleep. I'll be right next door in the living room. If you're hungry later, I'll order something." He kisses my forehead and says, "If you sleep through the night we'll talk tomorrow."

I undress and avoid looking at myself in the mirror. I throw away the pads I had lined the inside of my bra with to absorb the leakage. My breasts hurt. I step under very warm water and I press to get some milk out and relieve the pressure. Somehow the heat helps. I wash my hair and appreciate the seemingly endless supply of water.

I dry up and slip in Ten's T-shirt and then in Ten's bed. I rest my head on a pillow and it smells like him, sweet and comforting. It's only 6 p.m. according to the clock on the nightstand but Ten is right, I'm exhausted.

I wake up in a jolt. I feel like my head hit the pillow three seconds ago but according to the clock it's been more than five hours. My breasts are so tense I think I'm about to explode. Ten is in the bed next to me. It's weird. I mean on our little corner of the beach in Long Island I have laid next to him hundreds of times but I've never been in bed with him. He's turned on the light in the bathroom and left the door slightly ajar. I love him so for thinking of little stuff like that.

In the dim light I can see that he's on his side leaning on one elbow looking at me. What's really strange is that he's not looking at my face. He's looking a little more south. I follow his gaze to my breast region and realize the front of the shirt is soaking wet. I'm leaking. I should have worn a bra and padded the inside with toilet paper. I forgot.

"Does it hurt?" he asks.

I lie. "Just a bit. It's not that bad. Well it wouldn't be if I didn't mind feeling like they will soon both burst. "Eventually it will pass. I just have to wait it out."

"I think I know of a way to help," Ten shyly says.

"You do?" The surprise in my voice is unmistakable.

"Yes, but I'm afraid your going to think I'm a freak."

"Never, I would never think that about you." I take a playful tone and add, "I know you're a bit weird. I mean seriously, you picked me as your best friend so you are weird but a freak, no never."

"Okay, so close your eyes," he says.

My trust in Ten is such that I do close my eyes without hesitation. I don't open them when I feel him pulling the T-shirt up to my neck.

I shudder when I feel that he's putting one hand on a breast and his lips to a nipple. It works. It's amazingly soothing. The relief is almost instant. I put a hand on Ten's head and run my fingers through his hair. I let him work on the first breast for a minute and then pull his head to the second.

I open my eyes and look at him. His eyes are closed and the expression on his face is so intense I don't know what to make of it. He's right. What we're doing would probably look freaky to others but there is no doubt in my mind that it's an act of pure and absolute love. It's amazingly intimate without being sexual. I close my eyes again feeling as if I had cheated by taking a peek at his face. He pulls away and with the most tender voice, he asks, "How are you feeling now?"

"Much better, thank you."

He cradles me in his arms and rolls on his back taking me with him.

"How did it make you feel?" I ask looking up at his beautiful face.

He thinks for a moment and says, "Trusted and loved. Lovey, you always made me feel loved."

I close my eyes and think about that Christmas day on the pier. One look at each other and we had known we had come with the same purpose in mind. We were tired of the games the grown ups were playing and we wanted to get off their crazy merry-go-rounds.

I go back to sleep thinking how lucky we are to have found each other that day.

Chapter 10

Ten cracks the kitchen door open and asks, "Is everything ready?"

"Yes, almost," I answer. "We still have time, the party is starting at eight."

"You're sure I can't do anything to help?"

"Nope, you have finals in a couple of weeks, you need great grades to get a summer internship in a top law firm, I don't want you in *my* kitchen," I growl back.

"Leave the girl alone, if she doesn't want help, you should thank the Lord and count your blessing," says a deep baritone male voice.

"Oh no Andy," I say. "There's a misunderstanding here. I did not say that I did not want help, I just said that I didn't want Ten's help. He's got some studying to do. Now your help would be greatly appreciated, Officer."

Ten retreats and calls out to Andrew, "There goes another opportunity to keep your big mouth shut, Officer Andrew."

Andrew walks in the kitchen and give me his best salute, "Reporting for duty, Ma'am."

Andy loves goofing around and never misses an opportunity to make me laugh. I give him a pile of ashtrays to scatter about the living room and instruct him to return for a more delicate mission when this one is accomplished. We need to push the furniture around to make a dance floor. I boss him around for a little while and when everything is ready, I promise him that when he finally decides to take the sergeant exam I'll be catering to his every need to make sure he gets all the studying time necessary.

I go to my bedroom to get dressed. I'm working so hard that I'm the lightest I've been in years. Nevertheless, without clothes on I feel horrible. Eve's pregnancy has left stretch marks all over. With clothes on, I look okay. No, the truth is I look good. Between Eve's birth in September and this New Year's evening I got myself back together. Tonight, I'm breaking in new black leather pants and a black silk shirt. Both were presents from Ten for Christmas. He also gave me a necklace with big black pearls that used to belong to his grandmother. She loved custom jewels and this one was of really good quality since it held up all those years. Otherwise Jane Clark wore very little real fancy jewelry. I remember she had a simple gold wedding band and then a ring with a sapphire and two little diamonds. I put the necklace on and look at myself in the mirror. I'm thinking that I'm looking pretty hot for a size 14.

Except that Alexander is the only one I would really like to look sexy for. I walk out of my room and Andrew whistles, "You look good."

I smile and curtsy, "You don't look too bad yourself."

Instead of the usual tee-shirt, he's tucked in a crisp white shirt in his jeans and it suits him. He's holding a tumbler of scotch in his hand and has a dreamy look on his face. This means trouble. The man can't hold his liquor. It's a good thing he seldom drinks.

"If you were not spoken for, I would seriously hit on you."

My smile vanishes. Why did he have to make me think of Alexander? Xander Wild is still in Europe. The last concert of his tour was yesterday. Tonight it's going to be a year since we parted. I haven't even spoken to him once since.

I don't care what Andrew says, as far as I'm concerned, I'm not spoken for by anyone and especially not by his brother.

If I'm to believe Andrew's drunken banter, Alexander still thinks of me as his girl and expects me to be waiting for him. If that's so, why hasn't he called me? When I think about it there are big bubbles of anger that pop to the surface of my feelings.

I catch Andrew in a hug and say playfully, "Well, your brother's not here and if you don't try anything tonight or soon, before I find a special someone, you'll never know if you missed your chance."

Andrew holds me at arms length with a mock horror look on his face and says, "Xander would rip my balls out, make me cook them, and feed them to me if he caught me just ogling you. Seriously, don't even let him find out that we share the same bathroom and that I walked in on you as you were showering!"

"You what?"

The intercom buzzes and Andy runs to answer it, "Saved by the bell," he says.

"We're not finished with this conversation," I say.

"Yes we are. You know he makes up things when he drinks," says Oliver.

"Oh good, you're home. I didn't hear you come in. Are you okay? » I ask him.

Oliver is our other roommate. He's doing his intern rotations and usually when he gets home he just crashes.

"Yes, Mum." Oliver often makes fun of the way I mother him but I think he secretly loves it. Who wouldn't, I would love to have some one taking care of me the way that I take care of them. I'm being unfair, Ten is always attentive and Andrew and Oliver are always caring.

"The last shift was quiet, I was able to catch a little shut eye," he says. "I'll be fine."

Ten steps out of his room as I walk to the kitchen get some ice out. I turn around and watch my three musketeers ready to greet our guests.

"Are we ready to party?" I ask.

"Hell, yes!" the three of them say.

Our friends arrive and soon enough we have a joyous party. I've had one of the cooks at work help me prepare a cold buffet so now that I have it set out I'm all done. Oliver's prepared a tape alternating fast and slow songs.

Couples are dancing in the middle of the room. When the slow songs come on, he dims the light and catches one of the cute interns he's invited. I watch them dance until I hear one song I love. It's *My First, My Last, My Everything*. Ten catches me and makes me dance. "I've decided that this is going to be our song, so you have to dance with me," he says.

I look up to him and as we move slowly to the rhythm of the music and my heart swells. "Did I ever tell you how much I love you?" I ask him.

"About a million times," he jokes.

"I don't know what I would have done without you."

"Shush," he says, pressing my head on his chest. "I probably need you more than you need me, Lovey."

I really can't imagine what my life would have been without him. I understand that I bring him all the love the little boy in him has always been craving but I'm not sure it's half as life defining for him as what he's done for me. Ten's my savior, he's my rock. He even gave me the self-confidence I badly needed to apply for a job I never dreamed I could get. Without him I would not even have presented myself to the interview to become Marc Martin's assistant. I had never heard of the restaurant entrepreneur before Ten showed the ad to me.

Ten had done some research about him and found out that, just like me, he had started out in his family restaurant. He had run away and found his first job at sixteen on a luxury cruise ship in New York as a low hand assistant.

Ten was right. Marc Martin was the sort of man that would hire a girl my age with no formal education but an experience similar to his.

Working with him for the past two months has been mind blowing and I have Ten to thank for it. So Ten's given me my job as well as the place where I live and the company of my wonderful roommates.

There's only one thing missing in my life. I need someone to fall in love with and forget Alexander. I need this so badly it hurts. When I think about Alexander it's like there's a ball of lead in the middle of my chest and I can't breathe.

This is just what's happening to me as the next song begins. It's a slow ballad Alex wrote about a girl. In the lyrics, he swears eternal love using my words "No one, no one ever before ... and I wish for no one, no one ever after."

The first time I heard it I wanted to die.

"I know you miss him, Lovey," Ten says, "but you know he's a musician, hell you even gave him your blessing to go on tour. You can't blame him for being away."

"It's over. If he were not over me why wouldn't he call me?" I ask Ten. "I know he calls his family. He's even called here and spoken to Andrew. Why not me?"

"Probably because he doesn't feel that the telephone is an appropriate way of communicating with you," Ten answers.

I shrug but Ten won't let go, "He's taken your family name

as his for a stage name. He's written wonderful songs about you. Do you know how many girls would kill to have him write about them the way he writes about his love for you?" He's right. The one we wrote together has yet to be released but the one we're dancing to is beautiful and I believe he wrote it for me using my words for him.

I just wish Xander Wild would come back home from his tour so I could have my Alexander back. I heard Andrew say that his tour just ended with his concert in London yesterday. He'll be home soon and the very thought of possibly seeing him again makes me shiver. The music goes back to a faster beat and Ten lets me go. I'm back playing hostess and checking on everybody.

I hear retching as I walk by the bathroom. I knock on the door and try to turn the handle. The idiot throwing up in the bathroom has locked the door. "Go away. Leave me alone." *Shit, it's Andrew.*

I go to the kitchen to get a thin skewer to slide in the central hole of the handle and force my way in. I find an unconscious Andrew and lock the door behind me. I pull his head from the toilet and push him against the wall. I take a towel from the shelf and put it under the cold water. The smell in the room is horrible.

I flush the toilet, kneel in front of him to wipe his mouth, and then some yucky stuff from his hair. Gross! I fold the towel in two and put it on his forehead. He's got a big gash. He's probably knocked himself out against the toilet seat in a heave. His eyes flutter open and he looks at the locked door and at me.

"How did you get in?" he asks. His speech is a bit slurred.

"I slid under the door," I answer and watch him try to process that piece of information. It's funny because he stares at the bottom of the door and then at me as if he's actually considering my answer as a possibility.

"Come on Andy, upsy daisy, I'm taking you to bed," I tell him as I get up and pull him by both arms.

"I'd love to do you," he says, "but I'm serious. Xander would kill me."

"I don't think you're in any shape to do anything but your pillow," I joke as I steady him in a vertical position and open the door. I walk him to his room and make him sit down gently on his bed. I unbutton his shirt which is covered with half digested stuff. I fold it in a ball using as few fingers as I can and then pull his shoes and socks of.

Had I ever entertained anything romantic with Andrew, I would be cured of it for good. I'll ask Oliver or Ten to come finish undressing him later. I make him lay down on his stomach with one hand flat on the floor. I've been told it can help with the spinning.

It's almost midnight and everyone's eyes are glued to the television showing the time square crowd. Everyone's eyes except Ten's, he's scanning the room looking for me. When he sees me he smiles and I rush to be next to him so by the time we're done counting down I'm in his arms and we both wish each other a happy new year.

1980 has to be better than 1979.

I look for Oliver but he's nowhere to be seen. I can't see the intern he was dancing with either and the door to his bedroom is closed. They're having their own private celebration. My mind goes back in time and I scold myself. Not tonight. Tonight I will not be melancholic. My life is good and I'm going to enjoy it.

Another hour and all of our friends are gone. I'm cleaning up when the doorbell rings. Ten runs for it and opens the door to a very handsome man who grabs him and kisses him passionately. I want to look away but I can't. It's the first time I see two men kissing and I'm fascinated. I want to ask Ten why he didn't invite him to our party but I never get the chance.

The guy winks at me and says, "Hello, you must be Lyv. Happy new year to you, little girl. I'm stealing your boy for the night." He steps back in the hallway and leaves with Ten.

I sure hope he's living in the building otherwise Ten's gonna catch a serious cold.

I have to stop being so protective. Protective, right. I need to check on Andrew. I do and, sure enough, he's thrown up again. At least he had stayed on his stomach and didn't suffocate. When will he learn he just can't drink?

I go back to house cleaning for a while and then decide I can't let him sleep in such a mess. I change from my leather pants and silk blouse into an oversized tee shirt from Ten's closet and return tackle Andy. I finish undressing him. He's in a stupor. I hope it's the alcohol he consumed and not a brain injury after the shock. I get him almost vertical and coax him in the bathroom. I set the water to a reasonable temperature and step in the shower with him.

I almost laugh to myself thinking that I'm pretty sure my three month old baby must be less trouble to manage than the three supposedly grown man I'm mothering.

Now that Andy's cleaned what do I do with him? I can't put him back in his bed because it's revoltingly dirty. I'm going to play musical beds. I'll put Andy in my room and go sleep in Ten's room.

I wrap up an almost naked and wobbly Andy in a towel and he becomes very talkative as I dry him off. Since he's watched me in the shower, he's got a fantasy starting with him washing my hair. So being together under the shower was like a dream come true except that I was wearing this stupid tee-shirt and that he's too drunk to get it up... Too much information. When he sobers up, I need to get to the bottom of this watching me under the shower story.

My bringing him in my room and tucking him in my bed is making him even more confused. He's apologizing profusely and telling me that for sure tomorrow he won't have this technical problem anymore. "Oh, I'm sure Andy," I say. "Tomorrow, your penis won't be the problem. It's going to be your head."

I turn out the light and retreat to Ten's room. The wet tee-shirt falls to the floor of Ten's bathroom and I fall in his bed. Boy, am I tired, I think I'll sleep all day tomorrow.

Chapter 11

I'm dreaming about the restaurant I'll be working in next week when a voice interrupts my dream. Oliver's voice is amused and curious "Hey Lyv! Wake up. The doorman buzzed. You have a visitor. I went to wake you and I found Andrew sleeping in your bed so I decided to ask Ten where you were and I find you here."

It's too early for him to wake me up. It's too early for anything but sleep. I pull the quilt over my head. "Leave me alone, too complicated to explain now," I mumble from under the quilt.

Proving that his hearing is really fine, Oliver laughs and says, "I don't give a damn where you sleep. I'm just giving you a heads up because the some one coming up may want an explanation. So if you don't have one ready you better think about one real quick."

Now I'm curious. I pull my head out from under the quilt and open my eyes. Early day light fills a corner of the room as I did not bother to shut the curtains last night. Oliver is standing by the door in his underwear. I squint and, yes, they're inside out. Funny way to start the New

Year. Especially for him who is usually so meticulous about his appearance.

In my half asleep I wrack my brain trying to think to whom I could owe an explanation. It can't be the Ice Queen, Ten's mother is somewhere exotic for the holidays. It can't be James senior, he's in Acapulco for the winter. It can't be Ten's boyfriend because he's with Ten and it can't be Ten because he wouldn't care that I slept in his room. Actually he would be relieved that I didn't put a puking Andrew in is bed!

My mind is too foggy from lack of sleep so I give up and ask, "Who are you talking about?"

The door bell rings and Oliver turns around without answering. He walks out leaving the bedroom door ajar.

I hear him open the door and say, "She's in Ten's room... don't ask me. I don't know. I don't care, I'm going back to bed... Oh and Happy New year."

Now I'm wide awake and there's this bubble of hope that grew out of nowhere. The only other person I could owe an explanation to is Alexander. Could it be him? I want to run out of bed to check it out but I'm naked. Instead of running, I close my eyes and pray. When I open them again, the door is open wide.

"Is it really you or am I having a dream?" I ask sitting up with the quilt wrapped around my bust.

"Waddaya think?" he asks. He smiles, walks in the room and closes the door behind him.

"If you're not a dream, I think you should lock it," I say.

He chuckles and turns around to twist the little knob in the door handle. He drops his bag on the floor and his coat on Ten's desk. He takes three steps to the bed and sits facing me. I run the tip of my fingers on his face to make sure I'm not dreaming that he's really here. It's much more pleasant than pinching myself.

I want to be mad at him and yell, "Your brother is my roommate. Andrew told you I had your baby and yet you did not reach out to me. Why didn't you call me? Why didn't you write?" but the only think I say in a whisper is, "I've missed you so much."

He puts his hands on my shoulders and draws me to him. His lips reach mine and I'm whole again. His kiss is so tender, even more than before. Or maybe I forgot. I feared I had lost him forever. I want to be his, whichever way he wants me. I hold on to him with all my strength. I'm filled with an irresistible need of him.

My hands are on his belt and then on the zipper of his pants. I feel his legs moving. He's kicking off his shoes. He breaks the kiss to pull away his sweater. He pushes his pants down and tears open a condom that looks like it just magically appeared out of nowhere.

I scoot over to the center of the bed to make room for him. He gets under the quilt and positions himself over me. He buries his face in my neck and thrusts himself inside me. I gasp. It hurts. My head is more ready than my body. He freezes for an instant and waits until he feels me relax. When I do, he stops holding back, he thrusts into me once, twice and the third time he roars "You're mine, all mine." Then he shudders and crumbles in my arms. Frustration doesn't even begin to describe what I feel right now.

I must have growled because he laughs and apologizes. "Sorry Love, I couldn't hold on. I promise, after I get some sleep, I'll make it up to you."

He tries to roll to his side but I hold on to him, "Please stay," I pray. "I need you right here."

"I'm not crushing you?" he asks.

"Yes you are but I love it. It makes me feel alive again," I answer. That gets a chuckle out of him. I'm glad someone's finding my frustration amusing. I'm finding it... frustrating. He relieves me of some of the pressure by leaning on his forearms. I look at his face and run my hands through his hair. It's much shorter than last year. Gone is the thick dark mane I could grab onto. "What happened to your hair?"

"In October I shaved it," he says.

"Why would you do that?" I'm curious. I know the man's a little vain and I don't see why he would give up his beautiful head of hair.

Looking a bit sheepish, he confesses, "It was a promise I made to myself. When you vanished I promised myself that if you came back, I would sacrifice my curls."

"Oh, that is so incredibly sweet," I say pulling his face down to mine. I kiss the tip of his nose and his eyes and his chin and finally I nibble on his lower lip. He's almost forgiven for his thirty second fiasco. "I've never stopped being yours, even if I failed you."

"Why do you think you failed me?" he asks.

"Because I let them take your daughter away from us," I say. My eyes are filling up with tears and I blink to chase them away. I want today to be a happy day but still I can't help myself so I tell him, "I'm so, so sorry, I tried as hard as I could to fight for her but I failed you, I failed her, I failed myself."

"Shush. We still have each other and we can make another baby anytime. Just say the word and we'll do it."

"Really?"

"Really *but* I have a confession to make," he says. I study his face as he searches for his words. I have no idea what he's going to say.

"Love, you have to understand that your baby, I'm sorry, our baby, is an abstraction for me. I never saw her, I never even saw you while you were pregnant. Hell, I didn't even know you were pregnant before Andrew told me about it in October. I just knew you had vanished while I was on tour."

He stops and thinks. "Anyway, what I'm trying to say is that no matter how much I care for you, I can't really share your grief."

He rolls to his back and I rest my head on his shoulder as I try to wrap my mind around his explanation. The logical part of my brain accepts that what he says makes sense. He can't miss Eve when he's never even seen her. She's can't be as real to him as she's real to me. Still, I'm hurt that he doesn't share my grief. It creates a distance between us. Ten understands and he mourned the loss of the baby with me. Why can't Alexander feel anything for her?

I scold myself and think that, on the plus side, he's also saying he's ready to be a father if I want another child. I need to sleep on it because I can't think after only five hours of rest. Obviously he needs to sleep as well because he's already snoring. I close my eyes and go back to dreamland.

I smile thinking that when I'll wake up I'll be cashing a ... sperm check?

Chapter 12

I'm happy. My life is perfect. I'm almost afraid to think that. I fear I'm going to jinx myself.

Well, it's perfect if I don't think about Eve. I still think of her everyday but I'm learning to deal with the pain and to let go of my anger against the Bitch. Anger and hate are too energy consuming and there are so many more productive things I can do with my life.

So yes, my life is perfect. I have a job I love, I've got a home, a real home. Not just somewhere I go at night to sleep. I have a place I belong to where I spend time with my family. It's an odd family made up of four fabulous guys I'm differently crazy about.

There's Ten of course. He's a little less available these days because now that he finished his term finals, he's making up for lost time with his downstairs lover. He's not brought the guy back home yet and won't tell us his name but I got the dirt from the doorman. Giovanni is a model and a would-be actor who lives most of the year in Italy. I don't know what to think of Ten being so protective of his relationship. Could it be that he's in love or, just the opposite, that they're just sex pals?

Then there's Oliver. He works and studies like a mad man. He's changing departments again soon and is still undecided about what specialty he'll pick. I'm rooting for obstetrics but that's because it would suit my own personal agenda. It would be nice to have an OBGYN on call at home because we're trying to have a new baby. An emergency specialist would be cool too.

The cute little intern we met in December has come back a couple of times but so have a few others. As far as we're concerned they're all called "Babe." It makes our life easier. Some days I think he takes the concept of rotation through the hospital too literally.

There's also Andrew, Alexander's brother who still apologizes profusely for the way he behaved on New Year's eve. He denies ever seeing me naked in the shower and argues that it was the liquor talking. I'm not so sure but I've let it slide. He's made the resolution to stop drinking anything stronger than beer. I tell him to study to become a detective or a sergeant. I keep nagging him because he says he's not happy. If he liked being a patrol officer I would leave him alone but he bitches about it all the time and doesn't do anything to change it.

Last there's Alexander who moved in with us at the beginning of the year. He has to stay put in New York at least for the next three months doing studio work with his band before he goes back on tour. He's very busy with recording sessions and I'm busy with work so we're not crowding each other.

Right now I'm finishing this fabulous restaurant renovation project as the first assistant to Marc and he has decided that now that he's sixty he won't work on weekends anymore so my schedule is not as bad as when I started. I now get my weekends.

Last Sunday I spent the day in the studio with Alexander. After everybody left we recorded the song we wrote together a little more than a year ago; just him at the piano and our two voices. I was so excited when I listened to us afterwards. I think the song is perfect with two voices. He needs to find a good female performer to put the song in his next album. We've got a date tonight but it's been a very long week and the only thing I really want to do is to go to bed and not hang out in some smoke filled bar.

As I enter our place, I call out "Anybody home?" I go to the kitchen to get myself a glass of water. I'm very thirsty these days. I'm trying to remember if I was thirsty when I started expecting Eve. I don't remember but then I hadn't even realized I was pregnant then. The apartment is totally silent. Strange, usually on Fridays at 6 p.m. everybody's home. Maybe Alex's studio time got extended and he's taking advantage of the extra hours. That's cool, I'll nap and maybe then I'll be ready to party.

I open the door to the bedroom and find Alex sitting at the foot of the bed with his elbows on his knees and his head in his hands. I close the door behind me, kick off my shoes and climb on the bed. I kneel behind him to massage his shoulders. The recording sessions can get very tense and this usually soothes him.

"Hard day?" I ask.

He stands up as if my hands were burning coals on his back. I look up at him. "What's wrong?"

"Everything," he says with a defeated look that I've never seen on him.

"Everything?" I don't understand.

"Yeah, what part of everything don't you get?" he barks at me.

I don't answer immediately but take a deep breath and count to ten in my head as I process what's being said. That's a trick Marc Martin taught me at work when he realized I had one single spontaneous reaction to aggression, I fought back. It's like I've spent all my 'flight' answers living with the Bitch. Now I will no longer retreat, I can only fight back with the rest of the world.

Marc's method is working. I take my second breath and keep on counting in my head instead of screaming at him that *everything* can't possibly mean what's going on with the two of us. Alexander drops to his knees on the bed in front of me and puts his hands on my legs. He looks at me as if I'm a puppy he's dropping at the pound to be put down.

"I'm so sorry Love," he says and my heart stops beating. *Everything* doesn't mean everything. It means us. My heart starts pumping again and the blood throbs in my temples. I open my mouth and gasp for air. I think that my soul just shattered in small pieces. He doesn't love me anymore. All my insecurities come back at the speed of light. Sure he's wanted me but no more. The only reason he's ever chased me was because I was the one that got away. I got away twice. He was really challenged because the second time I did get away in a spectacular fashion. Now, I'm here, all his, totally available, the magic has gone.

I close my eyes and bite back the questions I want to ask. Were those weeks of total bliss for me, weeks of total hell for him? I won't say a word. I have to spare myself the humiliation. I want to run away and hide but I have nowhere else to go. This is my home, this is the place where I'm supposed to be safe. I thought his arms were my shelter. Was I totally blind? Why am I this stupid? I blink repeatedly to make sure I don't cry and press my lips together to remain silent. I'm afraid if I open my mouth I will howl. I swallow hard. I have to keep some dignity.

"Say something Love," he says. I shake my head and sit back on my heels. If I can't run that means he has to go. I don't have the strength to ask him to leave.

My hands are resting on my thighs and the only thing I can see is how big I am. It only takes a few seconds for the wave of sorrow to wash away all the self confidence my belief in Alex's love had given me. I don't have anything to say. If it's over, it's over. I'm not going to make a spectacle of myself.

I barely hear him when he says, "I love you. I think I'll always love you. You're the sweetest woman I know and I don't want anybody else but you." The words reach my brain and they're not making any sense. I look up to his face. I don't understand. How could what we have be wrong if he feels that way about me? He must read the question in my eyes because he tells me, "It's this domestic life I can't deal with."

I hear the explanation he's giving me but I don't believe him. It's not even been a couple of months since he's moved here. We've both been so active that there has been no time to create a boring routine. I understand the fear of the wear and tear of a relationship. I get it. Really I do. I know that the magic of the beginning eventually fades with the passion. I've always been a people watcher so I know this happens. I have no illusions. Curiously it seems that living with a wicked witch prevented me from believing in fairy tales. Unlike regular teenagers, I know happy-ever-afters are few and far between. But I believed we would have one because we were not ordinary people, because our love was deeper than most.

I can't understand what the issue is. We're living very privileged lives. We both do something we love, we're both becoming successful at it and there's been no money issue. Just as Oliver and Andrew do, I pay my share of the maintenance and utilities to Ten and I've never asked Alex for a penny. There's no drudgery. How could he possibly be unable to deal with our domestic life?

The only explanation is that he's having second thoughts about us having another child. He's scared of committing to me. He's scared by the responsibility of being a father. I just wish he would tell me the truth instead of taking the coward's way out and making up this stupid excuse. He gets up from the bed and I think he's going to leave but instead he goes to the door to lock it shut, takes his clothes off and then comes back on the bed next to me stark naked and obviously aroused. I want him so badly the idea of pushing him away barely registers in a far back corner of my mind. I know I should but it seems like the most absurd thing I could do right now. If this is our last time together I will take it and make the best of it. I'm pitiful.

Tonight I have back in my bed the Alexander of the first night. He's trying really so hard to please me as if he wanted to spoil it for anybody after him. He's tender and delicate and so loving that his caresses are almost painful. There's not a single part of my body he doesn't explore and bring to life. Every cell tingles and catches on fire under his touch.

He doesn't only take care of my body magnificently making up a hundred times for his return debacle, he messes with my brain as well by saying all the right things. All the words that I want to hear pass through his lips. He tells me how much he loves me. He swears he can't imagine how empty his life would be without me. He whispers that I have this magical power over him, that when I look at him I give him incredible strength and that it's only because I love him that he feels he can conquer the world. His words and his touch make me soar like I never soared before. I rise to heaven again and again and when I think I'm done and sated he lifts me up one more time and I let him. I don't ever want this night to end but at some point I can't keep my eyes open and I fall asleep in his arms holding on to him for dear life.

A few hours later, I open my eyes. His guitar case is no longer tucked away behind the door. He's gone. On the nightstand there's a tiny blue square box and an envelope. A parting present? A goodbye note? I don't want to open them. I push them in the top drawer of my nightstand and slam it shut.

I want to go back to sleep and believe, he's just gone out of town for a gig and he'll be back tomorrow. I roll to his side of the bed and bury my head in the pillow that smells like him. He said I was his harbor, if he really meant it he'll have to come back to me, won't he?

Chapter 13

What's wrong with this picture?" Marc asks me as he's paying the check for the meal we barely touched. I know this is a test. If I pass, Marc is going to let me tackle my first take over. I'll be one of the new managers at Marc Martin Restaurant Extraordinaire, Inc.

"What do you want me to start with?" I ask.

He shrugs, "It's your show Lyv."

Okay, it's sink or swim time. I warm up by stating the very obvious about the restaurant we just had a very unimpressive meal in. "First there's the location. This place is smack in the center of a very busy part of town. There's a great potential for lunch and happy hour. I'm not sure about dinner."

Marc nods and I feel a little more comfortable when I go on. This is my world. I know how it works.

"Second there's the decor. It stinks. It's horrible. I understand not every one shares my taste for bright and airy and that dark, intimate does have some charm but this is like a funeral home."

Marc chuckles. He obviously agrees.

I continue. "Without even turning bright lights on I can tell that the place should not pass sanitary inspection. Everything if filthy." I show him the color of my napkin. I used it to wipe the fold between the seat and the back cushion in our booth and you can tell no one's thought of cleaning it in like ... for ever. Marc makes a face and shows me his napkin. He's done the same on his side of the booth and it's just as revolting.

I go on about the staff. "They're very obnoxious, actually they match the food. It's obnoxious too." Marc raises an eyebrow. I defend my choice of word. "Yes, food can be obnoxious when the presentation on the plate is a lot more interesting than the flavor of the content." That gets a half smile out my boss. I go on for a while more and there's no doubt in my mind the only thing this place has going for it is its location.

I stop and look at Marc expectantly. He shakes his head and asks, "So you like the place we saw yesterday better?"

"No doubt in my mind, the other one requires only minor work. It could be done in less than two months. There's just some rethinking of the decor and maybe some retraining of the staff. I think it has a lot going for it and I sure can't understand why they went under."

"I'm glad you feel that way because I purchased it this morning and you're starting the renovation on Monday. Of course you need to finish the renovation and start it running before your due date. Do you think you can do that?"

I swallow my emotions and say, "Yes, Marc. Thank you. I won't let you down." At the same time I cradle my tummy with my hands and send a silent prayer to my baby. *Honey, don't you even consider coming early.*

I can't believe I am so lucky. Not only did Marc agree to give me chance when I was so very young but he's kept promoting me and never batted an eye when I told him I was expecting. The most amazing thing is that for sentimental reasons, his corporation is subject to French law and that he's applying French law rules to his American employees.

For most of those I work with, the down side of this is that we get paid monthly instead of weekly. I never had a pay check before he hired me so I don't see what the big deal about this monthly pay is, but it seems it takes some getting used to for a lot of people who were used to get their money at the end of each week.

But no one really complains too much because we also have a health plan, three weeks paid vacation, and the cherry on my cake, a month fully paid maternity leave. You've gotta love the French and their protective laws!

I decline Marc's offer to drop me home. It will do me good to walk a few blocks before I get to the apartment and crash. Ten wants to take me out to go celebrate my 18th birthday but I'm too tired I would rather stay home with my boys. I can't believe that I'm only nineteen. Nineteen and pregnant again. Sounds like the title of those horrible novellas they gave away at Sunday school to make us fear temptation. Well I got tempted and I sinned and I'm not repentant.

I haven't heard from Alex in many months. I have made Andrew promise that he wouldn't tell him about the pregnancy. Ten drove the point home by telling him that if he lets it slip, he's out in the street. Since there's no way our favorite police officer could find such nice accommodations for the price he's paying, his family loyalty is no longer a top priority. There's more than one way to understand that charity really begins at home.

It takes me forever to get back and when I finally do, I'm greeted by the most delicious smell. This is great since I barely touched what was served in that restaurant from hell. If the restaurant's dining room is dirty, chances are the kitchen is not very clean either.

I kick of my shoes and tiptoe barefoot in the kitchen. Oliver and Ten are cooking. Oliver's latest conquest is sitting on the counter top with a glass of wine in her hand giving them instruction on how to destroy the lumps of their gravy. Wow, they're making gravy? I have this sudden craving for a mashed potato volcano with a spoonful of gravy lava. What's wrong with me? I use to have sexual fantasies, now I have food cravings. I'm eighteen pushing sixty.

Three pairs of eyes turn to me as I step in and Ten asks, "So?"

I pull from behind my back the bottle of Champagne that I purchased on the way home and say, "Yes! I got the promotion. You are now talking to the new Marc Martin Restaurant Extraordinaire property manager and," I pause for effect, "I got a new property to put in shipshape before mid November."

They all cheer loudly and Ten says, "Congratulations, Lovey."

Oliver takes the handle of the saucepan from Ten's hand and starts giving a serious beating to the mixture. I think it works. The lumps are so intimidated by his natural authority that they vanish. Ten applauds in awe of such culinary talent and Babe scoots down from the counter to go stand very close behind Oliver. She slides her hands into his front pockets and I look away. I know precisely what she's doing and it's not fishing for spare change. I hope she doesn't get Oliver so distracted that he'll let the gravy burn.

Ten bends over to speak to my belly, "Now baby, you're gonna be real good and you're gonna stay put till the due date."

As the two of us, well three I guess if I count baby, get out of the kitchen. I laugh and ask, "How do you like being a father figure?"

He grins. "I can't wait and that's something I want to talk to you about."

"Can we talk in my room, I'd like to put my feet up?"

"Sure. I'll be with you in a minute."

I plop on my bed with my butt on one pillow and my feet high on the headboard. I close my eyes and start to devise a battle plan in my head for the work that's to start Monday on the new place. I've been first assistant for renovation on the past three projects. I should be able to make it work. In a perfect world I should be able to reopen during the first week of November so I'll shoot for that and give myself two weeks of wiggle room. I would really like a few days to rest before I'm due.

Ten walks into my room, laughs at my position and sits down next to me, his butt on the other pillow and his back to the headboard so we look at one other.

"This is not how I had planned to do this but I guess I'll have to rough it," he jokes. "Lyv Wild," he says. I'm startled. He never calls me anything other than Lovey. This must be serious. "Will you marry me?"

He presents to me a little jewelry box. Inside there's an exquisite ring with a blue stone encased between two small diamonds. I recognize the ring, Ten's grandmother used to wear it. I'm so stunned, I don't know what to say. I bring my legs down on the bed and kind of kneel in front of him. I look at the ring again and then at his face and try to make sense of what I've just heard.

"Lovey, it's not some crazy idea that just crossed my mind," he explains. "I've been toying with it for a while. Actually it was Granny who planted the seed."

"Granny?" The woman's been dead for ages.

"Yep, when I started fooling around with girls and brought them home to make my father and grandfather happy, she asked me what I was doing. First I wondered if she thought I was favoring men and was wondering why I was not coming out. Still I was not sure it was what she meant. She was a liberal and all, she did have a couple of gay acquaintances like her hair dresser and the decorator she hired to furnish the model homes when she was in charge of sales of the Clark homes, but I could not believe she would be okay with a bisexual grandson. Anyway, just to make sure, I asked her," he smiles sweetly as he remembers the conversation.

"She said that she did not understand why I was fooling around when I had already found you. According to her, you were the perfect girl for me. She said that she understood that maybe I was not in love with you and that I loved you as a friend but according to her that was perfect. She said a marriage based on trust and friendship would actually be more solid and last longer than one initially based on passion."

I have fond memories of the old lady and I knew she liked me but I had no idea she thought so highly of me. "I have to think about this," I say.

"Fair enough."

I bounce the idea of being Mrs. Clark around my head. It springs one major question. "What kind of marriage are we talking about?"

Ten understands what I'm asking perfectly. "A real one, Lovey. If you'll let me, I will start by being the father to this little one," he gently puts a hand on my belly, "and then, in a few years, when you're ready, I would like for us to have more."

He slides down to take me in his arms and continues, "You'll move to my bedroom and we'll convert this one into a nursery. We can get an au pair to take care of the baby when you go to work and then we could ask Andrew to move out to make a room for the next baby and then again, when Oliver graduates, we'll have another room for yet another baby." Ten's given this a lot of thought and already has it all planned while I'm still grasping at straws trying to look at my best friend in this new light.

"Of course, if the good doctor doesn't finally get settled with someone, we'll have to make sure he doesn't bother the au pair girls..." he jokes.

"So we'll be lovers?" I ask. I know it's silly because if we don't there won't be any babies but I still need to ask.

"We will," he says and adds, "I'll have to figure out how to do it right for you."

"That's silly," I say punching him lightly, "you've been with girls before."

"Yes but I didn't really care for their needs at all. I was very selfish in bed," I gasp. My heart goes out to those poor girls.

"I don't want to do that with you. I want to make you happy. I want to hear you moan and scream louder than you did it with Xander when he lived with us."

I'm turning red. Was I really that loud that all the guys listened in? I guess I was. "What about men?"

"What do you mean?"

"At some point you'll probably want a man again, don't you think?" I say.

"Probably but if you can resist Xander when he comes back, I should be able to resist men."

"He won't be coming back," I protest.

"Oh yes he will." Ten makes it sound like it's a done deal, like Alexander's return is as certain as the return of the tides or the seasons. "In his own twisted way he does love you, you know. The second he hears that you've agreed to marry me and that you are sleeping in my bed, he'll come running back for you."

He may have a point. Little boys can be very possessive about their toys. Even those they no longer wish to play with. Because the toy's been discarded doesn't mean that someone else can play with it.

"Mark my words. Your turning him away will make him even crazier about you. It may be hard on you," Ten says. Yes it will. Just thinking about Alexander hurts.

"I'm the best man for you, Lovey. We've been a pair for the longest time. You know that you can rely on me and that I will never let you down. You know I love you. I'll be a good father for our children and that includes Eve if we ever find her."

I think about it and try to look at Ten in this new light he's casting on himself. "If I marry you," I say, "we'll have to be brutally honest with one another. No lying, no cheating. If I commit to you I will never go back on my word but I will ask the same of you. If it ever becomes too hard for you, I want you to tell me before you stumble so we can work it out or set each other free."

"So you'll think about it?"

"Yes I will. You need to give me some time to get used to the idea. I'll tell you in November, after my opening night. Is that okay for you?"

"Sure. Will you let me cheat a little to help you warm up to the concept?" he asks sheepishly.

"What do you mean?"

"Will you let me kiss you?"

"Why would that be cheating?" I ask amused.

"Because I've been told I'm an amazing kisser."

He's grinning and I can't help but laugh. "I don't know about kissing yet," I say "but I already know you're going to be an amazing lawyer. You just sold me on the kissing. Now I'm dying to know what I've been missing out on all those years."

Ten leans me back on the bed and finds a comfortable position next to me. He adjusts his long frame around my round belly and when his lips get close to mine I close my eyes. The entire concept of Ten kissing me like a lover is so foreign it's mind boggling.

What's even more startling is that his kiss is not gentle. Where Alex was a tender explorer in awe of discovering unchartered territories, Ten is a conqueror scorching the earth on his way. He bites my lower lip and then as a king warrior takes possession of my mouth with his. There's nothing tentative about his kiss. He's taking charge and it's so overwhelming that when he pulls away I draw a gasping breath.

"This is who I am in the bedroom. I'm generous but I'm also very demanding and bossy and direct. If you say yes, I expect you to surrender to me."

I look at this new side of Ten I've never seen before. I'm in shock. Good shock.

He looks at me intently and explains, "Out of bed you'll remain my best friend. We'll be partners and you'll own my soul. In bed, I'll be your boss and you'll be my plaything."

I gasp. God, I don't know what's with me. I think his bossy nature is sexy. This could work. I could learn to love him differently.

The hard look vanishes from his face and, looking very happy with himself, he gets up walks around the bed and offers his hands to help me stand, "Come on, Lovey, let's go celebrate your promotion. There's roast beef, mashed potatoes with gravy and pecan pie."

"Oh, I so love it when you talk dirty to me," I say and he roars with laughter.

Chapter 14

I tackle my project with a new strength. Marc's trust in me is a real booster. I don't want to let him down. Being one year older also helps. Since my return from Florida I was afraid the Bitch would file a missing persons report and that one morning the police would come knocking on our door and that Ten would get in some sort of trouble.

As the months passed my fears dissipated but now they're completely gone. I'm officially an adult in charge of my own life. It's exhilarating. Of course this is not the life I had planned but who gets to live that life. Well, Oliver maybe. He always wanted to be a doctor and that's what he's going to be.

But I'm going to be okay even if I never go to college because Marc is giving me a better education in restaurant management than the one I could have received at any school. It's totally hands on and, instead of spending thousands of dollars to get instructed I'm getting a pay check and health benefits. What more could a girl want?

My life is good. I shudder. The last time I had such positive feeling Alexander walked out on me. I shrug my shoulders and chase my dark thoughts away. My life is good and it will stay good because I have Ten by my side.

I gather my crew and tell them about my plan for the renovation. I have a dozen guys working for me this week, all recruited by Marc. Ten jokes about my team. He says even if he were the jealous type, he wouldn't be worried about what could happen to me at work. If one of the guys takes my dress off it will be to try it on he says. He's exaggerating but he's not totally wrong.

My boss is not simply gay, he's flamboyantly so. He's totally unapologetic about it. I'm not sure if it's his French upbringing or the incredible success he achieved at a young age but it's like he doesn't care what people think, while at the same time, part of his success is tied to his image. Somehow his bubbling and extreme personality makes it work. So Marc strongly favors hiring gay men and claims that gay construction workers are the best because they have the strength of a man and the attention to detail of a woman.

This makes for a closely knitted community and the work atmosphere is so intimate that I actually know that two of the guys in my crew are into crossdressing. Yet I very much doubt they would be interested in trying on a maternity dress!

The guys start pulling the horrible velvet from the wall while I sit at a corner table studying the place's accounting. At the end of the day, the walls are stripped bare, ready for a nice shiny coat of washable paint, and I know why the place went under while it had almost everything going for it.

The staff has been robbing the owner blind. The numbers on the books for the last two years don't match the results of the last three weeks and the only thing that changed during those weeks was that we had the restaurant under close supervision with one of Marc's people at the cash register and Marc supervising the orders. During those weeks it was impossible for anybody to doctor the orders and the receipts, obviously the way they did before.

There's more than thirty percent difference in the results! A close examination shows that the numbers for the bar have not changed significantly so I know it's the cook and the headwaiter who were in cahoots. They probably had private deals with the suppliers. No wonder the poor guy filed for bankruptcy and had to sell his restaurant. Those two employees have to go.

Now whether they should go to jail for this is a totally different kettle of fish. Marc will decide if he wants to give this information to his seller or to the D.A. Yep, sending some one to jail is way over my pay grade. Back home, I talk about this with Ten. He agrees with me. This is not my responsibility.

For once Oliver and Andy are on the same schedule as we are. The four of us have dinner and Andy raises his hand like a schoolboy requesting permission to speak. We stop talking and look at him.

He blushes a little and seems to hesitate so I ask. "Did you register for the sergeant's exam?"

He shakes his head.

"You passed the sergeant's exam?"

He shakes his head again.

"Enough. Spit it out," Oliver says. I laugh because he has zero patience. Maybe he spends his entire quota at work and has none left for us at home.

"Alexander called."

Ten glares at Andy and the silence is deafening until Ten hisses something that I don't catch between clenched teeth. Andy ignores him and continues, "He'll be back in town next month and he'll be one of the guest stars at the annual Smart and Sharp charity concert on November 8th."

"Good for him," I say. That means that in two years he's become a real star.

"Yeah, it's cool, right?" Andy says. "Anyway he wanted to know if we would come. He said we'd have VIP access and backstage passes. You know, all the works."

Ten bangs a fist on the table and growls, "You've got to be kidding." I can't figure out if Ten's really mad or if he's just trying to convince Andrew that he's mad hoping that he'll convey the message to Alexander. I don't think I've ever seen him that way.

I put my hands on Ten's arm, "Shush, you've awoken the baby." In a second I have three pairs of hands on my tummy feeling the baby kicking.

Andy smiles and takes his best Irish accent to say, "Hey Lass, you've got a soccer player in there."

Ten says, "I'm rooting for a ballerina."

"What's your expert medical opinion?" I ask Oliver.

He laughs, "You're not getting me in the middle of this but whatever it is, this is healthy kicking."

Now that I have Ten calmed down I say to Andy, "Thank Alexander for me but tell him that I won't go. November 8th is the tentative opening date for my restaurant."

"I have no intention of going either," says Ten.

Andy doesn't look surprised. "That's what I thought but I needed to ask."

"Well I'll go," Oliver says. "Back stage passes sound like fun and maybe I could take a girl there with your pass." That's my Oliver, always looking for a new way of scoring.

"Xander Wild has two songs in the top charts," Marc tells me as we're walking through the kitchen for a final inspection before the opening.

"Yes, I know. He's made it now. He's playing at the big charity concert tonight."

Marc looks at me with curiosity. The man can crunch number faster that any calculator so deducting nine months from my due date has not taken him more than a second.

I'm pretty sure he remembers that, at the time of conception, Alexander was the one who came to pick me up at work when he kept me really late. Marc also noticed that it's been a while since he's seen Alexander whereas Ten has often dropped by on the site to take me home. I can see he wants to ask me about my situation but he thinks better of it.

Like me, he loves to know everything about everybody he works with. He's a great source of information because he loves to gossip. That's why I won't admit anything about my situation to him. Oh well, chances are I will eventually tell him but for now I enjoy watching curiosity eat him up.

When the restaurant opens, he stands by the door, greets all the guests, and takes all the credit for my hard work. I'm not sure how I feel about that. On the one hand, I did do most of the work but then again, he's trained me and he's paid for all the renovation so the truth of the matter is, it's actually his creation. I decide to be gracious about it. Tonight it's his most absolute right to claim my work. I'm let him parade like a peacock. Next time I'm sure I'll try to steal some of his thunder.

I hang around, sitting on a bar stool making sure there are no glitches. I'm so big I can't really do anything but supervise. At ten Marc sends me home in a taxi.

"I don't want to hear from you before you're back home with the baby," he tells me.

Amazing, I'm on maternity leave! I told Ten I would let him know my decision tonight. I pat my tummy. I hated not having a father, I wonder how my child will feel if he or she ends up with two dads.

I don't have the time to enter my key in the door that Ten has already opened it for me. He takes my coat and closes the door behind me.

He looks like he's on pins and needles. It's plain to see that he thinks I've tortured him long enough. His eyes scream to me that I have to let him know now. Like right this instant. I nod to him and he tilts his head silently begging me to say something out loud to make sure that there's no misunderstanding, that I'm really saying yes. So I say it.

"Yes, I will be honored to become your wife Mr. Tennessee Charles Clark."

He drops to his knees, wraps his arms around my thighs and kisses my belly. "I love you already," he says to my belly button and his playfulness brings tears to my eyes.

He jumps back to his feet, takes my hand and brings me to his room. "Voilà!" he says as he opens the door.

His masculine, brown queen size bed set has been replaced by a California king size bed. His alarm clock and his reading lamp are on the floor on the side of the bed he usually sleeps in. On the other side there's a pretty bassinet covered with white lace.

I'm speechless.

"I thought you would like to pick the headboard and the night stands," he says. "But I wanted a big bed where we'll be able to cuddle with the kids."

I'm laughing and crying at the same time. Only Ten does that to me. The baby's not born yet and he's making plans for the next one, no, the next ones with an emphasis on the plural. "You know I love you," I tell him.

"Yes I do," he says. "And I'm giving you a new opportunity to prove it."

"Your wish is my command now that you're going to be my Lord and Master," I playfully answer.

"Come with me to Long Island tomorrow to tell Gramps and my parents. Correct me if I'm wrong but I don't think you want a big wedding, right?"

I shake my head. He's right. I've never dreamed of the white lacy dress or of the nuptial march and all that jazz regular girls dream about. I don't have any family and I was never allowed to have many friends when I grew up so I couldn't even fill the tiniest chapel. Maybe it's not so true anymore if I invite everyone I work with. For a second I have this cute vision of Marc walking me to the altar with a feather scarf around his neck, but no, a big wedding is not my dream.

"That's what I thought. So here's the plan, on Monday we'll get our marriage license and we'll do it on Wednesday."

"Did you also pick our witnesses for us?" I joke.

"Sure did. Oliver and Andy, unless you have someone else in mind."

"No I don't. I think you made a good choice."

"So it's a yes?"

"Yes, as long as you don't plan to take me there on your bike or to make me eat at the Main Street Diner. Yes, I will go help you face the Ice Queen. Now I just want to brush my teeth and lay down." Actually what I badly need to do is pee. Someone's been kicking my bladder.

I step in his bathroom, in our bathroom, and sure enough my toiletries have already been moved from the bathroom I used to share with Andrew. He smiles at me and I refrain from asking him what he would have done if I had declined. The question would be cruel and I don't want to burst his bubble. The Ice Queen will work on blowing it soon enough.

When I get back in the bedroom Ten helps me undress and for the first time I feel a little self conscious with him. I need to buy a nightgown. Just as the thought crosses my mind, I see it. On the bed, he has prepared something for me to sleep in tonight. It's the T-shirt I slept in on my first night here.

On the nightstand there's the jewelry box with the ring and Ten kneels in front of me to slide it on my finger.

I really love that man. I pray to fall in love with him.

Chapter 15

The estate is empty when we arrive in Oliver's car. I was dead serious about not doing the ride on the bike. Anyway, I think it was not really an option; the only way I would have fit would have been side saddle. We wait in the living room for the family to return from the Sunday brunch pilgrimage. I wonder about the Ice Queen latest passion. I guess I'll see it soon enough.

The room conjures up memories. When I look at the piano, I can see myself sitting next to Alexander on the bench writing our song. I look away and then I realize that I can't look out the window either. When I do I see the hot tub. This is where Eve was conceived. I search for something safe to look at and set my gaze on the engagement ring on my finger. Ten's grandfather gave it to his wife to celebrate their 25th wedding anniversary.

When her arthritis had made it impossible for her to wear jewelry, Ten's granny had put that ring in an envelope and told her husband, "It's for Tennessee. He'll know what to do with it when he comes to his senses."

After his grandmother passed, Ten's grandfather gave Ten the ring and the message without making any comments.

If he had questions, James senior had kept them for himself. My guess is that he had no questions. His wife probably had told him what she thought.

Ten paces back and force between the sofa on which I'm sitting and the window overlooking the gravel road that leads to the house. When they finally arrive, he appears to be a nervous wreck.

I get up and go stand beside him. I thread my fingers in his and ask,, "Are you okay?"

"Sure, it's just an awkward moment but I owe it to Granny."

Ten steps in front of me as if to shield my body with his when his grandfather enters the room. "What a pleasant surprise," he says to Ten. He does not hug him. The Clarks are not huggers. "Oh, and Lyv is with you. It's been..." James Senior is speechless. If Ten wasn't so tense he'd be amused. I never thought something could throw his grandfather off his game. The old man turns around and speaks to his son who just walked in.

"It seems that your mother was right after all."

"What are you talking about?" James Junior asks. Then he recognizes me and ascertains my condition. He stands there with his mouth open.

"She predicted *that*?" he asks.

I would like to gloat and say, "Yes, James, your mother knew your son would end up with the help," but that wouldn't be very productive or mature.

James Junior just stares at me until his father makes him

snap out of his stupefaction by suggesting he get his wife to join our party. "She should be here with us and not with her charlatan."

As his son follows his instructions, James Senior chuckles and says to Ten and me, "The man is the most expensive astrologist she's had yet and guess what, he never saw this coming while it's very obvious my dear, you didn't get this way overnight."

"It took about eight and a half months," I say. In the right context sarcasm is a weakness of mine.

"Right, what I said, a charlatan."

"Tennessee Charles Clark, what have you done?" The Ice Queen's voice is shrill. She's about to loose it and I can't say it's making me sad.

"Well I would say that's pretty obvious," her husband tells her.

"Maybe it's been so long that she's forgotten," mumbles James Senior.

Oh my, I'm contagious, we're having a sarcasm fest. James Senior gives me a hard look and asks, "How long has this been going on?"

I turn to Ten and let him answer this one. "I've always loved her," Ten says.

James Senior looks at me and I nod. Yeah, what he said. I've always loved him too. Probably not the way we want you to think we have but we're not lying about our feelings.

"Then I guess you kids know what you're doing and you have my blessing."

"Thank you sir," I say.

"Well they certainly don't have mine," says Ten's mother.

"Alexandra! For once in your life, would you please shut up!" The woman looks flabbergasted. She huffs, at a loss for words, and storms out of the room.

I pinch myself. I can't believe my ears. Ten's father has suddenly grown a pair. I look at Ten who seems as surprised as I am by this show of courage.

"Are you married already?" Ten father's asks.

"Not yet but we're planning on doing it before the baby arrives. Probably on Wednesday," Ten tells him.

"Would you mind if we came?" James junior asks.

Ten looks at me. He obviously had not considered the possibility that they would want to be there.

"Of course not, Sir." I say. "We would be delighted if you were with us."

"Good, then just let us know where and when," Ten's father says and just leaves the room. I guess this is as emotional as he can get.

James Senior is laughing as he watches his son walk out calling out for his wife. "Well that was interesting." He raises his glass in my direction and says, "Welcome to the crazy dysfunctional Clark family my dear. You have no idea what you've gotten yourself into." Oh but I do. I had the chance to observe them every Sunday morning for years. Ten turns around and looks at me.

He says, "I think we're about done here Lovey. What do you say we drive back home tonight?" I nod. It's not as if we had a choice, we haven't been invited to stay for dinner. Of course we could stay the night, Ten still owns the bungalow but I think I'll feel better at home.

"Goodbye Sir, it was a pleasure to see you again."

I start walking out and then I think of something and I turn around. "May I ask you something?" I ask the old man. He nods.

"Is Martha still working at the diner?"

"Yes she is," he answers.

"Then could I ask you a favor? Next Sunday, when you see her, can you tell her that I'm doing fine and that I think of her often?"

"That I can do," he says.

"Out of my mother's hearing?"

"That goes without saying." He smiles when he says that. I guess he really noticed more than I gave him credit for; unless there's something between him and Martha that I'm not aware of.

We get in the car and Ten holds my hand as we drive away. "It went better than I expected," he says. "I'm glad we did it."

I lift his hand to my lips and say, "I love you, Ten."

Keeping his eyes on the road, he asks me, "Do you miss Alexander?"

"At times." I say. One of the rules we have set is to be brutally honest, so I'm not about to start lying to him before we have tied the knot.

"We'll have to work on that," he says. He's smiling to himself. There's a competitive side to Ten that I'm seeing for the first time. I look forward to his best effort to make me forget Alex.

"Yes, we will."

I haven't gone for the virginal white. Given my size it would have been silly. Furthermore I don't think they do white maternity dresses in the winter. So even if I had wanted to it wouldn't have been possible.

James Senior and James Junior are here. They drove all the way to Manhattan to be with us. Ten was surprised, in a good way I think, to see Clara, Jimmy, and Steven. There is no one representing my biological family and nothing could make me happier.

Oliver and Andrew are our witnesses. Those two and Ten are my family now. I guess Alexander still is too.

Andrew's in the middle of his shift but he got the green light from his supervisor to take one hour with his patrol car to be with us. Who knew his sergeant was a romantic at heart? The cute clerk seems favorably impressed by his uniform. Andrew looks at her with such intensity that I think he'll be back to visit this courtroom soon and that I may get to know her better.

The ceremony is quick. We both say, "I do," and sign the paper.

I'm now officially Mrs. Tennessee Charles Clark. Ten kisses me, for real. Long and hard. So long that Oliver coughs and says, "Get a room!" and starts to walk away with Andrew.

And then, with a perfect sense of timing my baby decides that it's time to come out and see the world. I get the first contraction and I feel something hot trickling down my legs. I recognize the pain the very second it starts. My grip on Ten's arm gets stronger and he looks at me with alarm.

"Don't panic please," I tell him, "but it's time."

Ten stares at me and calls out to Oliver and Andrew standing by the elevator doors. They both turn around and walk back toward us when they see the tense look on Ten's face.

Oliver start's to say "What's..." and then notices the small puddle on the floor between my legs. His voice is really cool like it's no big deal when he continues by saying "Okay, since your water broke, I'll be starting my shift a bit earlier than usual."

"And I'm gonna get you there in style," Andy tells me. "Lucky for you I cleaned up the back of my patrol car yesterday."

"Sorry guys, we've got to go," Ten says to his family.

"What hospital?" Clara asks.

Oliver tells her as we get in the elevator.

In the patrol car Andy turns on the siren. The three of us are a little squeezed in the back. More warm liquid comes out of me.

Oliver laughs and says to Andy, "Buddy you're gonna have to clean your car again."

"Oh Lyv, please can't you do something to hold it in?" Andy asks.

I can't help but laugh. The man has no clue about the way things work. I'm not peeing in his car, I have no control over the leakage.

This time I'm not scared of giving birth. I can conquer the world! I have my musketeers with me.

But the three musketeers were actually four buddies and today one's missing. I decide not to be sad that Alexander won't be with me. I know it's going to be all right because Ten's here.

Chapter 16

Andrew drops us at the entrance of the hospital and drives away. He's got a shift to finish and a back seat to clean up. Again. Ten has the number of his desk sergeant who will radio him the news if the baby gets here before he finishes his shift, which seems unlikely. I hope this baby doesn't take as much time as Eve to come out.

Andrew drops us at the entrance of the hospital and drives away. He's got a shift to finish and a back seat to clean up. Again. Ten has the number of his desk sergeant who will radio him the news if the baby gets here before he finishes his shift, which seems unlikely. I hope this baby doesn't take as much time as Eve to come out.

Oliver rushes us through the admission paper work and in a semi private place, it's a pre-delivery room. Ten's holding my hand and he doesn't care what anybody says, he's not going anywhere.

I no longer have contractions. Ten's worried until Oliver summarizes the situation for him in words he can understand:

"She's not in labor, she's just leaky."

Ten's brain seems to have stopped functioning properly.

"He means you can relax, nothing's happening for a while. You have plenty of time to go home and get my stuff," I say using a tone I would use for a very slow person.

"You're sure?" Ten asks.

"Certain," Oliver and I answer together.

"And I'll stay with her until you come back," Oliver says. "I told you, I'm not supposed to start work for a couple of hours."

Ten reluctantly leaves. I know he's really not thinking properly because in his normal state he would have sent Oliver home to get my baby suitcase.

Oliver stays with me and I can see something's on his mind so I tell him, "Come on, out with it."

He looks at me strangely so I add, "I can see something's bothering you so tell me. What's the problem?"

"It's Andrew. He's torn."

"I know…" It's all that I can think to say. Andrew is in a difficult position. He's there because of a combination of his brother's decision and my choice not to tell Alexander about this pregnancy.

We remain silent for a while and Oliver says, "If there's anything I can do to help?"

"You are already. You're here with me and you haven't spilled the beans."

Oliver shrugs. "My loyalty is to you and Ten. Alexander's not my brother."

But still I can see Oliver's feeling sorry for Alexander. So am I when I'm not mad at hell at him.

The delivery is fast and smooth and it's a girl. Ten looks at her before they whisk her away. "She's perfect," he says. "And she looks just like you."

"What shall we call her?"

"What do you think of Alexandra?" he asks.

"Alexandra?" What the hell?

He nods and I can't think of anything to say. I'm in shock and then I understand. It's not Alexandra because of Alexander. It's Alexandra like his mother. Okay, that makes more sense. I'm not sure it will melt the Ice Queen frozen heart but I won't deny him a chance to try. I wonder if he was hurt by her absence today.

"Sure," I say. "Alexandra is a pretty name."

"Then Alexandra it is."

Ten's family minus the Ice Queen comes to visit us the next morning. They crowd my room and go through the required "ooh"s and "aah"s and then James Senior asks, "So what's her name?"

"Alexandra." Ten's answer has his grand father snorting and Ten's dad all teary eyes. The poor man must still be in love with his dreadful wife who will probably never come and visit.

"I thought Alexandra Jane Clark has a nice ring to it," I say, keeping my eyes on the baby.

"Now you're talking," roars James Senior at the addition of his wife's name to the one of his detested daughter in law.

Ten bends over to kiss me and whispers, "Nicely played, partner."

After what seems an eternity, a nurse comes and chases them out. Ten accompanies them to the door.

I'm blissfully alone in my room and once the nurse has checked me out, I lower my hospital gown to start nursing Alexandra. I close my eyes and breathe in deep. There's this direct connection between the nipple and the shrinking uterus that is violent.

I finish nursing and Ten's not back yet. I guess his family is getting chatty. The door opens as I'm closing the nursing bra.

"Why?"

It's Alexander not Ten. He looks a mess. He stands at the foot of my bed and says, "I want to kill the bastard. He should have called me months ago."

I don't know if he's talking about his brother or about Ten but I don't care. I shush him, "Please lower your voice, you'll scare the baby."

"Why?" he asks again more softly.

"Why what?"

"Why didn't you let me know?"

"If you're joking, this is not funny," I say.

"Damn right, it's not funny. Didn't you read the note I left you?"

"No and I didn't open the box either. They are probably still in the drawer of my nightstand."

"You didn't even look at it? Why?"

"Because there is nothing that you could possibly have written that would have taken away the pain you inflicted when you left."

"But I wrote that I would always love you." It takes all my will power not to scream at him. "I wrote that I wanted to spend my life with you."

"Right, you said that to me that last night and then you waited for me to fall asleep to run out like a coward." I'm talking as softly as I can because of the baby. What I really want is to scream at the top of my lungs.

"There was more to it. I love you and you know that if you had told me you were pregnant again there was no way anyone could have kept me away. I would have done the right thing," he whisper-shouts.

"*The right thing.*" I repeat shaking my head. He nods frantically. "Oh Alex, have you ever understood anything about me at all?" He looks absolutely clueless so I guess not. I need to spell it out for him. "You know that I spent the first eighteen years of my life feeling unwanted and unwelcome *every single day.*"

He's listening intently, maybe for the first time, but he's still not getting it. "You realize that I hated every second of that life?" He nods. "Then how could you imagine I would consider for an instant living with a man who would stay with me because it was *the right thing to do*?"

Still, he's not getting it. "Alex, I want the man I live with to be by my side because he wants to be with me and not out of a sense of duty." There's a flicker of understanding in his eyes. Maybe, at last, he's starting to see my point of view.

"I want the man I live with to be happy to see me every morning when he wakes up and glad to come home to me at night. I could never settle for a man who will go through the motion while regretting some other life that he wished he could have had, and that's who you would have been." He looks broken but I'm too mad at him to let it go at that. "So reading your card couldn't have made a difference. Whatever it said you couldn't have changed my mind. You made it up for me when you left me."

"You should have read it, Love..."

I interrupt him. "And now you have no right to tell me about your regrets or to say that you feel miserable because you made your bed."

"And you can't call her 'Love' anymore," Ten says. How long has he been standing there? Alexander turns around and looks at Ten and then back at me.

"Fine, I won't call you Love anymore. But please, don't shut me out." He looks at his daughter and says, "I never got a chance to see our first daughter. Please, let me be a part of this baby's life?"

Ten looks at me and shrugs. I understand that he's letting me decide. My mind is racing. I want to send him away but then again I can't see myself denying him access to his daughter. He's not a bad man. He's just ... selfish and immature.

Ten looks at me wrestling with my conflicting feelings and comes up with a suggestion "He could be her Godfather." Alexander nods and looks at me.

I stare back at both of them. "I don't want us to lie to her," I say. They both frown at me. "Ten, you will be her father. She will have your name but she will be told that Alexander is not only her Godfather, that he's also her biological father."

Ten thinks for a few second and then nods. Alexander breathes deeply and says, "Thank you." It's not a perfect solution but then it's not a perfect situation either.

"What did you decide to call her?"

"We're calling her after Ten's mother and grandmother," I say.

"So what's her name?" Alexander asks again.

"She's Alexandra Jane," Ten answers and has an awakening when he sees Alexander smile for the first time since he's entered the room.

"Her Godfather approves, you couldn't have thought of a better name."

The look in Ten's eyes tells me louder than words that incredibly, somehow, he had not realized before this instant the irony of his choice.

"Alexander," I say. "I'm tired now, I would appreciate it if you left us."

"Of course, I'll be on my way. May I kiss her before I go?"

Without giving me a chance to answer he leans over our daughter and puts his lips on her forehead. He's so close that I breathe him in. Nothing conjures up memories more sharply than the sense of smell for me. His smell is so sweet, it's pure torture. As he raises his eyes to me, I shake my head and he knows better than to touch me. But the damage is done. Scar tissue is bleeding again.

Ten studies me as I watch Alex walk out. When the door closes he says, "Seeing him still hurts." It's not a question, he can see it my eyes.

I don't hide it but I let him know how much I believe in him. "I'll be fine. You're gonna make it all better. Right?"

"Yes, dear. I'm your husband now and it's my duty to make it better," he says. I think I see relief in his eyes. He's happy that I don't lie to him but still my honesty is probably hard on him.

THIRD PART
- 1981 À 1983 -

Chapter 17

There's this feeling of déjà vu as I look around the living room that we just finished getting party ready.

Déjà vu with a major difference. The 1979 Andy was already drunk at that time. The 1980 version of Andy is only lightly buzzed as he goes about placing ashtrays in the strategic places. True to his resolution, he's been drinking beer instead of scotch and the lighter drink agrees much better with him. There's another major difference. I'm no longer waiting for Alexander to come back home to me. The wait for Alexander is over. I'm with Ten now and tonight's the night.

We've been married almost two months and sleeping in the same bed. For the first month the most exciting thing I did was nursing Alexandra under Ten's watchful gaze. A few weeks later, after a check up, I reported that we had the doctor's green light for sex but Ten said it was too soon.

I was relieved and disappointed at the same time.

Ten's been a perfect husband in every other way. He is true to his word. He promised me that we would be partners and we are. He consults with me on all his important decisions and he's given me a power of attorney on all his accounts. I know precisely where we are financially and we're actually doing very well.

The fact that James senior is paying for the au-pair girl for the first two years does make our life a lot easier.

Ten has also been an open book about his past. The only thing he's been discreet about is Giovanni. He confessed, "He's my Alexander. I'll keep the scar of that relationship but the wound is closed."

Slowly the nature of my love for him has shifted. Sometimes I wake up at night and watch him sleep. I long for him to touch me. The more we wait the more I actually want him to want me. I realize he was right to make us wait.

Last week I asked him if we were ever going to consummate our marriage and he grinned at me in such a way that I understood it was what he had wanted all along. He had been waiting for me to ask him.

"How does New Year's eve sound?" he answered.

"Like an eternity away," I said and for my eagerness had been treated to a toe curling kiss. His erection was pressed along my leg and I almost reached out for him but then I remembered what he had said, "In bed, I'll be your boss and you'll be my plaything." I had to let him take the initiative and he had said New Year's Eve so I waited.

Every night since then there's been a lot of kissing and hugging and touching. He gets me all worked up and then, when I'm really hot and bothered, he says "New Year's Eve..."

The man is devilishly manipulative when it comes to sex.

So tonight there's a lump in my chest as I'm simultaneously looking forward to and dreading the last stroke of midnight.

Andy's totally oblivious to my state of mind. He's in his own bubble because he thinks he's going to score tonight. He's invited Mary-Ann, the cute woman that was in the judge's office when Ten and I were married. I had thought at the time that she was the clerk but she's turned out to be younger than I imagined. She's a college student working part time as an administrative assistant and not a law school graduate acting as a clerk.

She made enough of an impression on Andrew that he went back to haunt the courthouse everyday during his lunch hour until he ran into her again. He's been taking her out a lot and she's come by the house a few of times. I've had a chance to get to know her a bit. Mary-Ann hangs out with me while the men are watching some sporting events on television.

She's physically my polar opposite: blond with blue eyes

and porcelain skin. She's so tiny she looks fragile but she's stronger than she appears. She's working her way through college and I think she'll go for a graduate degree once she decides what she wants to do. She's been in the courthouse long enough to know that law is not her thing. She enjoys the legal reasoning but hates conflicts. Before that she worked in a veterinary clinic and while she did love working with the animals she couldn't deal with the owners.

"I've been thinking about my career choices," she tells me when I return to the kitchen where she's helping me preparing finger food. "I think I'm not a people person. I'm more at ease with abstract ideas than with real live situations."

"So it seems," I tell her. "You need a job that minimizes contacts with third parties. Maybe something in the field of research or you could become a writer. Writing is a very solitary exercise, no?"

"How do you do it?" she asks.

"Do what?"

"Deal with people all day? The restaurant staff, the patrons, the suppliers, your boss, how do you put up with that? And then you come home and you've got to deal with three men, an infant, and the au-pair girl. I would go nuts!"

"Really, you would?" She nods. "I've never thought about it

that way. I just enjoy working with people. I get a kick out of pairing talents. We're all a tiny part of a giant jigsaw puzzle. We need connections. When people click, the sum of what they can accomplish together is so much more that what they could all do going their separate ways."

She looks at me as if I were an out of space creature.

"I understand that some people would rather work on their own but we all need to bounce our ideas off someone after a while, no? What's the use of writing the most beautiful book if no one can read it? What the purpose of discovering some fabulous invention if you don't share it afterwards?"

The intercom interrupts me. The other guests are arriving. Ten opens the kitchen door and gestures for us to get out in the lobby with him. "Thank you for helping me and keeping me company today," I tell her as we walk out.

"It's always a pleasure to be with you," she says. "I have this tendency to see everything in black and white, I like that you make me notice shades of grey."

"If you stick around long enough, you'll even start to see colors," Ten says. "Lyv's greatest power is the one she gives to those she loves. With her by my side I know I can conquer the world."

My heart stops. Ten's words are identical to those Alexander said to me the last night we were together. I guess this is what they both see in me, someone that believes in them so much that they become invincible. I wonder how I do that.

I look at Ten and the affection I read in his eyes is mind-blowing. I put the tray I was carrying down on a table and go to him. "I love you," I say for the millionth time. I so want him to understand, to know for certain that he's not my second choice, my fall back guy.

"And I love you more than you know, Lovey," he says. There's a twinkle in his eyes and all my apprehensions about tonight vanish for an instant.

"You guys are going to make me sick," Andrew says and he makes noises as if he's going to vomit.

Mary-Ann playfully hits him and says, "I think it's charming that they are so in love and that Ten's not afraid to say it."

Andrew rolls his eyes at her but it seems he gets the message about showing affection since he grabs her hand. It's a beginning.

The evening passes in a blur and soon enough after we cheered in the new year, Andrew escapes to his room with Mary-Ann. Oliver won't be home for a few hours. He's a first year attending physician now and the first year docs get to pull all the holiday night supervision.

Ten's cousin Jimmy, his childhood buddy Steven, and the girl who seems to be their common girlfriend are the last to go. I'm happy that Ten is staying connected with them. I actually like them.

When the girl was out of ears' reach, Jimmy and Steven mentioned something about starting a family. I don't really understand how they're going to make it work but I'm all for it. Are there girls out there who are okay with living with two men for good? I hope there are because it would be nice if our kids had cousins.

I tip-toe into my old room where Ten has set up Alexandra's cradle. Tonight is a first for her as well. She's moving out of her parent's bedroom. She doesn't seem to mind. She's sleeping soundly. She's been sleeping through the nights and she'll be perfectly safe in here. That's what I repeat to myself as I walk out and close the door. I turn around and Ten is watching me from our bedroom. He holds out a hand to me. I walk to him and I take it.

"Come on, Lovey. It's time for bed."

He closes the door behind us and I say, "I'll be there in a minute."

I go to the bathroom and brush my teeth. As I get out of the bathroom he's waiting for me by the door. He catches both my hands in his and pins me against the wall with our arms up in the air. He looks at me so intently I close my eyes and shudder.

"What do you want, Lyv?" he asks.

I open my eyes again and whisper, "I want you, Ten. I

want you so much it scares me."

"Good, I want you to be mine, just mine," he growls as he nips at my neck.

"Then do it," I plead.

Keeping my two hands up with just one of his, he unzips the back of my skirt. It falls to the floor. He pushes my underwear down and I wiggle to make it drop further. His hand explores the apex of my leg and in a minute he has me panting.

I realize that I'll probably have bite marks on my shoulders and my neck for weeks but I don't care. I buck into his hand and moan. He brings me close and then stops to open his belt buckle with one hand. Close again and he stops for the top button of his pants. Oh so close and I whimper, "Please, Ten, don't stop."

He chuckles, "Patience, Lovey. We have our whole lives ahead of us, there's no hurry."

I let out a growl of protest and he silences me with a kiss. He takes over my mouth and with each flick of his tongue a piece of my will vanishes. My entire existence is limited to my reactions to his touch. The only part of me that remains is the mirror to his desire. When his mouth leaves mine to tear with his teeth the wrapping of the condom that he took out of his pocket, I'm consumed by my need to become one with him. My entire body arches up into him. He frees my hands and says, "Hold on to me,

Lovey."

I wrap my arms around him as he lifts my up. My legs are around him as he pushes into me. Trapped between the wall and him, I have this incredible sensation of lightness as he pummels into me.

What I feel is so intense, I'm afraid of letting myself go. I fear that if I do I will explode in so many tiny pieces that I will never be whole again. Somehow Ten must sense it because he says, "Come on baby, you're safe with me, let me take you higher."

That undoes me and I gasp back, "Don't hold back, my love."

His pace picks up and I do shatter in so many delicious directions that I totally lose control. But losing control again is fine. Ten is here whispering in my ears that he loves me and that he'll never let me go. It conjures memories of other tender whispers but I chase them out of my mind. I have a husband and I'm in love with him.

We rest, out of breath in each other's arms until Ten gently frees my legs. He holds on to me to make sure, I'm able to stand. I'm shaking like a leaf.

"Are you cold, my love?" he asks.

"No. Just overwhelmed by emotions."

Chapter 18

I enter the bathroom and leave Ten in the bedroom looking kind of funny with his pants half way down his legs and his hair all messed up. He's sexy as hell but funny too. I finish undressing in the bathroom and get back into our room wearing one of his T-shirts I've been using as a nightgown since we started sharing the same bed. He's gloriously naked, laying on his stomach, half covered by the bed sheets. His back is turned to me as he's setting up the cassette player by the bedside. He gets the machine started and it plays *My First, My Last, My Everything*. Barry White's deep voice makes the room cozier.

He turns his head around and looks at me.

"Take it off," he says with a commanding tone I've never heard before and that gets my heart racing. I take the hem of the shirt with my hands and pull it over my head. I let it drop to the floor by my skirt and resume walking toward the bed.

I'm very self-conscious. When I look at myself in the mirror the only thing I see on my body are the stretch marks left by two pregnancies. They have scarred my breasts and the lower part of my tummy from belly button to pubic hair.

Ten doesn't seem to see the marks. He holds out a hand to beckon me to the bed and says, "You're so beautiful, I want to look at you. You're never wearing anything in bed with me from now on."

His tone doesn't leave any room for discussion and I like that he takes control. It's funny because I'm really bossy. I take charge of everything all day. I would never have guessed I would love giving up control. Maybe it's a question of trust. Ten has never betrayed me. His love for me is unconditional so when he orders me around, I don't feel threatened in the least. Incredibly, it does feel sexy.

I smile, take his hand and slide under the covers in the bed next to him.

"When we're here," he says, "I want you to use words to respond to me if I ask you something."

"Okay," I whisper and somehow repress a nervous giggle.

"I will be very demanding and I need to know that you will obey my orders or voice out your concerns or complaints if you have any."

I nod and he raises an eyebrow. Right. I have to speak.

"I've heard you," I say.

"Good, now come closer to me and stop shivering," he says. His tone is a little softer but there's still an edge to it. "Are you sure you're not cold?"

"No, not cold. Just out of my comfort zone."

There's this strange expression on his face as he says, "Good, I want you that way. I'm going to get such a kick out of keeping you off balance."

I gasp and he caresses my face with the back of his hand. "Don't worry Lovey, you're going to love everything I will do to you. You trust me, right?"

I almost nod and catch myself before I do, "Yes I do and the strangest thing is that I find this new side of you very hot."

"I knew you would," he says. "And in this room you're so going to enjoy being mine to pet. I'm going to make you my sex toy."

Those are words I've never heard him say before. He's never been crude like this and it unsettles me. I have no time to catch my breath as he spreads my legs apart and rolls over to kneel in between them.

"Put your hands under your head and under the pillow," he says.

I obey him as he continues. "Tonight is our first night so I will go easy on you but you can't touch me. It's all about me discovering what makes you tick. Another night, when I'm in the mood to let you touch me, you'll get your turn."

He puts his lips between my breasts and raises his eyes to watch me.

"I did not hear your answer," he says.

"Was there a question? I just heard a list of instructions," I say.

His mouth travels to a nipple and he bites me. Hard. Well not harder than Alexandra when she's nursing but harder than a lover would do. Well harder than Alexander did. Oh my God, no. I can't go there. I need to chase Alex from my mind when I'm in bed with Ten.

My husband's tone is not tender when he says, "I'll let it pass this time but you need to learn my rules. Don't get sassy with me."

I refrain an impulse to roll my eyes as I would with a temperamental child. I don't mind playing but he's got to be reasonable. I still have some free will... or maybe not, because his touch is like fire.

His hands are on my inner thighs. They journey from the knees up ever so slowly. I love it and I moan.

"Good, I like it when you do that. It's music to my ears. Let it all out. Don't hold back or hide anything from me."

I whimper. He leans toward the top of the bed and kisses me. His hands are on my breasts and then on my tummy and then he kneels again and goes back to the inner side of my legs so close from where I want them to me. He stares at me and asks, "How much do you want me Lovey?"

"More than I can say."

"Do you need me?"

"More than my next breath," I cry.

He reaches out for a condom on the night stand and sits down on his feet. He puts it on and then, with a finger light as a feather he finally reaches in between my legs. He presses ever so lightly around the sensitive nub and my hips shoot up to him as I gasp. "Please, Ten."

The finger slides down and explores my fold still swollen from our first session.

"Please, what?" he asks. His tone is so intense that I'm not sure what to say. He told me he was going to keep me of balance and I'm not sure I should tell him what I really want.

"Please enter me," I beg.

"So sweetly asked. I can't refuse."

He slides one arm underneath each knee and pushes my legs up as he lowers himself onto me. As he fills me this way I realize how big he is. I gasp again. He freezes and I make a little protest sound.

"Are you close?" he asks.

"So close."

"Good, show me," he says as he resumes his invasion of my body. It takes all of my will power not to pull my hands from under the pillow to reach out for him. He wants total control and I give it to him. As I explode again under his care, I think I'm starting to see the pleasure of surrender.

Ten rolls over to his side and gets up to dispose of the condom. He comes back in bed and pulls me over to him. I rest my head on his shoulder and he kisses my hair.

180 | Olivia Rigal

"Mine," he says with a sleepy voice. "You're all mine now."

I have a smile on my face. He's tender again. I may learn to love his bossy side but right now, I mainly crave his sweetness.

"And you are mine as well. I love you, Ten," I whisper. "I never thought it possible but I do love you more every day."

"I love you, Baby. I wonder why it took me so long to realize I wanted you for myself," he says. "If I had I would have spared us so much heartache."

"When did you figure it out?" I ask.

"I think I started to realize that maybe you were more than my best friend when you slept in my bed that first night. In your sleep you were calling for Alexander and that made me jealous..."

"But you were still with Giovanni then, no?"

He nods and says, "and then Xander came back and I hated his guts. I realized it was not fair and that if I had Giovanni you should be allowed to have Xander but still I resented him. I was so happy when he skipped town that I wanted to cheer. You were just mine again and I liked it that way."

I never noticed anything. At that period I was in my little bubble of joy. Obviously, there were tensions between my best friend and my boy-friend that escaped me totally.

"I have no regrets," I say and almost feel guilty saying it. I don't regret loving Alexander. The truth is I think I still love him. Funny how I can love the two of them at once without feeling loving one takes away from the other. I'm not saying it out loud but I know Ten would understand precisely what I mean since he loved Giovanni and me simultaneously.

"None what so ever?" he asks.

"Well, there's Eve."

"Yeah I know Lovey. Eventually we'll find her. Andy's sergeant has all of his contacts in Florida looking for her. With all those retired New York cops searching we'll get a lead soon."

Chapter 19

Lyv Wild?" The man's voice on the phone is familiar but I can't seem to place it. But then it's seven on Sunday morning and that's not my favorite time of day. I'm not sure I would recognize Ten's voice. But it can't be Ten because he's sleeping next to me.

I grunt, "Yes."

"Lyv, you've gotta come home," the voice says.

This doesn't make sense. I'm home. In my half sleep I can see through the door opening we made between our room and our daughter's room that Alexandra is in her bed. Yes, this is my home. Who ever this is has a stupid sense of humor. It's a bad joke. I need my sleep. "This is not funny," I say before I hang up the phone and then take it of the hook again.

Ten's half awake and asks, "Who was that?"

"Some dumb joker," I say. "Let's go back to sleep."

"I've got a better idea," he says and lifts the cover. Part of his anatomy is fully awake.

I laugh and say, "I see a bad case of morning glory."

He puts his hand on my head and doesn't need to push. I know what he wants. I trail down kisses on his chest and take my times going where he wants me to go. He growls a little but I know it's just for show. He's okay with my teasing him a bit. Not too long though. He doesn't want me to think I have any control over what happens in our bedroom. But sometimes we don't get what we wish for. For instance, I wish pancakes and maple syrup were diet food and I don't think it's ever going to happen.

He's been bossing me around in bed for more than a year now and the truth is that his bark is stronger than his bite. Still I do what it takes to get him to bite me every so often because his bite is oh so delicious.

When I get closer and just touch him with the tip of my tongue, his hips tilt forward and his hand becomes more pressing on my head. I put my lips to the mushroom tip and grab the bulk of him in my hands. He lets me pleasure him for a while and then he fists his hand in my hair and pulls me away.

I look up to him surprised. He's never stopped me before.

"Come up here," he says. "No matter how much I enjoy this, I know this is not going to get you pregnant, Lovey. I think it's about time we give Alexandra a brother."

I laugh. "What if we have another girl?"

"Nope, not going to happen. Did I not tell you I'm the boss of you in bed? If I say it's going to be a boy, you're gonna make me a boy," he's grinning as he says that. I know he'll take in stride whatever pops out but still, I now know he would favor a boy.

"If I do deliver a male per your heart's desire, my gallant sir, will you grant me one wish?"

"Whatever you want, my Lovey," he says as he pulls me over him to straddle him.

"We won't call him James. Please. There are enough James in your family."

"If you give me James as a middle name, you'll get to pick his first name."

"It's a deal," I say.

He lifts me by the waist and then pushes me down on him. I tilt my head backwards and all thoughts of name are gone. I'm just a ball of need and I concentrate on the friction of the most sensitive part of my body. Time stands still or it rushes by too fast, I can't tell. I'm lost to the world. Nothing else exists but Ten. He stops moving and slides a hand between us. Not so gently he presses my nub between two fingers.

"How good is it?" he asks.

"Amazing," I whisper, "You're killing me and I'm loving it."

I look at his face, "Don't hold back, Ten. Give me what I need to make you a beautiful baby boy. He'll be as handsome and smart as his Dad and the most loved baby on earth."

That undoes him and for the first time he doesn't balk at my command but jerks his hips up while applying more pressure with his fingers.

I swallow the scream that almost escapes me. I may be lost to the world but I still remember that the door to our baby girl's room is open. I crumble on Ten, panting.

He flips us over and slides a pillow under my butt.

"What are you doing?" I ask.

"Helping gravity," he says.

I laugh, "You're crazy you know!" but when I see the way he looks at me I know I crave that type of crazy. There's so much love in his gaze, tears come to my eyes.

"Are you thinking about Eve again?" he asks.

"No my love, I'm thinking how lucky I am to have you."

But now of course, I'm thinking about Eve again. I hope she's a happy little girl. I hope she loved and cared for. I think Ten can read this in my eyes because he kisses me with more passion than ever. He kisses me to make me forget all about Eve and, for a while, I do. The kiss lasts long enough for him to get aroused again.

"Are you ready for more?" he asks.

"Are we shooting for twin boys?" I tease him.

"I never thought of that. Sure two boys would be cool!"

I think not. One at a time seems enough work especially when there's princess Alexandra who requires 300% of our attention. One would never know that Ten is not her biological father. He's the best dad ever and Alexander is a dotting Godfather.

Alexander visits every time he's on the East coast. That's almost every other month because he travels a lot. He tries to come when Ten's not around. Maybe because seeing the way Alexandra adores her father tears him apart. It's kind of perverse that he comes so often. I think it pains him but he can't seem to stay away.

I try to make sure I'm not around when he hangs out with our daughter because no matter how much I love Ten there is no denying seeing Alexander still gets to me. I scold myself but I can't help it, I think about what might have been.

"Lyv," Ten says. "You're not with me. What are you thinking about?"

The man knows me so well sometimes I think he can read my thoughts.

"That with your spoiling of Alexandra, twins would be hell!" I'm not lying, just omitting part of my thoughts. I kiss him in the neck the way he loves it.

"Okay so one boy only it will be."

"One boy coming up," I call out as I would if I was sending an order from a kitchen restaurant and we make love almost playfully. Ten lifts me up in a bubble of pure joy and bliss. I think this is what happiness tastes like. We fall asleep to be awakened by Oliver a few hours later.

He knocks on our door and opens without waiting for an answer. Maybe he's been knocking for a while and realized he wouldn't interrupt anything. Alexandra is cradled in his arms eating who knows what. I think she's sucking on a piece of bagel. What time is it anyway? The clock on the nightstand says it's almost noon. Thank God for Oliver'crazy schedule and his love for our baby. Every so often he takes charge of her and let's us grab more hours of sleep.

"I need to make a call," he says, "and you've go the phone off the hook."

"Oh, right. Some crank call at the crack of dawn," I say. I pull on the cord and get the phone out from under the bed. I put the receiver back on its cradle and say, "There. Sorry."

Alexandra wiggles in Oliver's arms and calls for her daddy. Oliver drops her on the bed on Ten's side. "I've fed her but I think you need to change her."

Ten looks at me and I say, "Oh no, she asked for her Daddy. You're the diaper hero today."

Oliver laughs and the phone starts ringing as he walks out of our room. "I'll get it in the living room," he says. "I'm meeting my mother for lunch and I'm sure it's her telling me she's early and already waiting for me at the restaurant."

Through the door as I get dressed I hear him say, "Hi. Yes, the phone was of the hook. Probably the baby tipped it over... yes that's what babies do... of course I never did that, I was perfect... sure, I'll meet you there in two minutes."

Oliver has a strange relationship with his mother. He's always talking to her with a condescending tone. It's like he thinks she a dimwit he has to pacify. I sure hope my kids never talk to me that way. I would feel insulted.

The phone rings again and Oliver picks up after the first ring. I'm thinking it's his mother again who forgot to say something but after the initial "Hello," he remains quiet for a while and then he says, "Thank you for calling. She's not available right now but if you give me a number I will have her call you back as soon as she can... Yes. I understand... Mr. Mitchell, yes ... " Oliver repeats a 516 area code number and says, "Thank you, sir."

Then I understand why the voice was familiar. It was Dave Mitchell. The sweet man from Long Island that saved me from long walks so many times. What could he possibly want?

I walk out of the room. Oliver has hung up and he's standing in the living room with a disturbed expression on his face. He looks at me when I walk in the room and says, "You may want to sit."

"What did Dave want?"

"You know him?" I nod. "He was calling about your parents," he says.

My reaction is knee jerk. "I don't have parents, they're dead to me."

Oliver ignores me. "He called to say that there's been an fire."

And then I get it. "You mean now they're really dead?"

Oliver nods and takes a step in my direction. He's got a weary look on his face, he's expecting me to crumble at the news and wants to be able to catch me if I do.

I step away. "I'm fine Oliver. I'm really fine. They were nothing to me so don't expect me to mourn."

Oliver is startled. "The number is on the pad by the kitchen phone."

"Thanks, I'll call him. Go, run. Your mother is waiting," I tell him.

"Oh right, for a second I forgot. Are you sure you're all right?" he asks.

Ten steps out of Alexandra's room with a clean baby in his arms. "Why wouldn't she be?" he asks Oliver.

"Because the early morning call was Dave, Dave Mitchell from the Hamptons."

"Dave? The garage guy who used to fix your bicycle? What did he want?"

"To tell me that my parents are dead."

It's so weird. I don't feel anything. There's no sense of loss, no regrets. I realize this is not normal. I should feel something but I don't. There's not even relief. They've been dead to me since Eve was taken away from me. Maybe they were dead to me earlier than that. I will not mourn or grieve. I'm actually okay.

If I'm some sort of monster for being so cold and detached, then Ten's the same kind of freak because he says, "I guess we'll be able to spend some time in Long Island this summer," and then he nuzzles Alexandra's tummy with his nose and asks, "Guess who's going to the beach in the spring?"

Oliver is standing with his hand on the door handle and his mouth open in amazement. Such indifference to my parent's passing is beyond his understanding. Lucky for him. It means that unlike me, life gave him a set of lovable parents.

Chapter 20

I'm standing in front of a pile of charred wood covered by a bit of snow. I don't feel a thing. The only impression that comes to my mind is that it's a pretty desolate scene. I feel blissful indifference. This is all that is left of my parents' house. It burned down to the ground. An electrical fire is what the insurance report states.

Gone is the scale on which she made me step once a week to make me feel self-conscious about my weight, gone is the crop she used to spank me with, gone is the metal comb she used to pull my hair out with under the guise of making me look neater... It's all gone up in smoke. I can't think of anything that was in that house that I could ever miss.

After speaking to Dave and apologizing for hanging up on him, I waited till Monday and called the coroner. A very nice lady told me that they were able to identify them with what was left. Almost calcined bones I suppose. She told me that it would be better if I did not come to see their remains. She said something to the effect of keeping my memory of them as lovely as I could.

I almost laughed. That would be a tall order but the poor woman had no way to know. She gave me the number of the local mortuary and I ordered two coffins. I didn't know if I would get anything from them but that was all right, I was willing to pay for their funeral because unlike them, I'm no monster.

Ten is standing beside me, holding my hand. He states the obvious, "There's nothing left but the land."

"That's okay. I wouldn't have wanted anything anyway. Ours are the only good childhood memories I cherish." He squeezes my hand. I know he understands.

"You're still getting the plot of land, possibly the insurance money for the house and then you'll also get the diner," he says. "Oh and there's the balance of a bank account. The banker said they had some nice savings."

Ten's been acting as my attorney and inquiring about the estate. I'm surprised the Bitch didn't leave it all to some charity to make sure I didn't get anything. My guess is she thought she still had many years ahead of herself before she had to get organized to make sure I didn't get a red cent from her.

"I want to sell everything," I say.

"Don't you want to think about it first? What about Martha? What about Wendy? They're still working there you know."

"I'll sell to someone who will agree to keep them on. I'll have it put in the contract," I say.

"We can do that."

"Thank you. I would like never to hear about it again."

"What will you do with the money?" Ten asks. "I have no idea what the diner will bring but the land is worth some nice cash."

I look at him with a grin and say, "Maybe it's time I spread my wings and start my own restaurant."

"Or you could stay home to take care of the kids. You don't need to work anymore. I can support us all."

It's true. He may not be getting as much income as he would have if he had joined a major firm but he's doing okay in the small firm he's picked. It's been his choice. He decided he would work more reasonable hours to compensate the fact that I often work at night. I frown and wonder if he's still happy with his choice.

He watches my change of expression and shrugs, "Just letting you know it's a possibility. You can do whatever you want, Lovey. I want you to be as happy as I am."

I smile at him and ask, "You're really happy?"

"I wouldn't trade my place with anyone else," he hugs me. "I just want a few other healthy babies and life will be perfect."

"God, Ten. How many is a few?" I ask.

"At least two or three more?" he says tentatively. "I hated being an only child. If it hadn't be for my cousin Jimmy and you I think I would have died of isolation."

I squeeze his hand and say, "Let's go one at a time but two more sounds reasonable. I'm not sure Alexandra would agree though. She's already jealous of any attention you give to me. She'll got bat shit crazy when you take care of another child."

"No she won't, I'll tell her it's a plaything, she'll believe that we made her sibling just for her."

I laugh. He loves her so much. I have to play bad cop most of the time otherwise we'll soon have a monster. We get back in the car. Ten's little princess is fast asleep. Car rides pacify her.

Tonight we're staying in Ten's beach bungalow. I'm dreading it because of the memories of Alexander it conjures but then the other choice would be the main house. I'm not sure I'm ready to cohabit with the Clark clan even for a night in a place that also holds memory of Alexander... Sharing the evening meal will be weird enough.

When we arrive we're greeted by Jimmy and Steven. They brought Laura with them. Laura is their live-in assistant. She runs their household and works for their auction house as well. They took her in right after high-school when she started college. She's studying art history. I think she's finished her masters degree and started a PhD.

She watches me get Alexandra out of her car seat and extends her arms, "May I?" she asks.

"Of course," I say giving my baby to her. "It's so nice of you to have come all this way to watch her while I attend the funeral."

"It's no bother at all," she says and there's a glow about her that I never noticed before. She's one of those women that looks good with a baby in her arms.

Jimmy and Stevens seem to agree with me. They have this warm way of looking at her twirling Alexandra around and babbling sweet nothings to her as she walks in the house. Alexandra likes her. Oh well, Alexandra likes anyone who treats her like she's the center of the universe and right now that's what Laura's doing.

Jimmy and Steven exchange a conspiratorial look. Yep, those two are ready for parenthood and up to something. They just need to find the right girl. And then I have a light bulb moment. They have the right girl. They're looking at her.

We all walk in the house. There's a nice fire roaring and James Senior is looking into it pensively. He turns around and says good-naturedly, "It's about time, I'm famished."

His two grandsons give him a hand to get up from the sofa and help him walk to the dining room table. He's aged a lot in the past six months and he's decided to live here full time. He seems to need a push to get started and then he walks like a wind-up mechanical toy.

The table is prettily set. Laura's work, no doubt about this. I notice there's a high chair ready for Alexandra. Jimmy follows my gaze and says, "I went looking for it and found it in the attic. It was mine and then Ten's."

"Mine," claims Alexandra and we all laugh.

"Thank you for digging up this family heirloom," I say.

James Senior sits next to me and puts his large hand on mine. "Now don't get me wrong, Lyv, I really like this little Alexandra Jane here but I would really love a great grandson. Do you think you could produce one before I kick the bucket?"

"We're working on it, Sir," I say.

Funny how he blushes a little. "Good, Good." He chuckles and says to Ten, "I have a confession and an apology to make to you, kid." Ten looks at him with a puzzled expression on his face. James Senior's not the confession type and he's usually unapologetic as hell.

"For years I thought you were batting for the other team," the old man says. "And since those two have this weird arrangement going," he points to Jimmy and Steven with his chin, "I thought the family would end with you guys."

Jimmy laughs, "We haven't said our last word yet. With a bit of luck we could deliver a great grandson before Lyv and Ten do."

For a second I think I see Laura blush and I see her in a new light. Wow, how does one handle two men? I look at the window not to stare at her nor at Ten who may be a bit uncomfortable and my eyes fall on the hot tub. I have this memory of one evening I spent in it, chatting away with Ten and Alexander. In my mind I try to play a film of me between Ten and Alex and it's so unsettling that I almost gasp.

Ten who is sitting between Alexandra's high chair and me follows my gaze and raises an eyebrow. I smile at him. Everything is fine. I think one man at a time is all that I can handle. But I do understand Laura. I know for a fact you can love two men simultaneously. I guess she's the lucky one because they're happy with that situation.

We finish dinner early and walk out through the cold to the bungalow. Some changes have been made since my last visit. There's a powerful radiator which warms up the place quickly and there's a gigantic bed that occupies most of the space. It's larger than a king size. I'm thinking it's been custom built.

"Since we were not coming around, I let Jimmy use it and you know..."

Ten doesn't finish his sentence but I get it. To be in a ménage you don't only need a bigger heart than most, you also need a much larger bed.

There's also a brand new child folding bed by the window. The price sticker is still on the bottom leg. In the bed there's a little pillow, the cutest blanket, and an old fashioned wood mobile. Laura has thought of everything. Obviously, she's ready to be a mother.

We put Alexandra to rest and she quickly falls asleep after playing with her crib toy. I'll have to remember to thank Laura for sparing me from the restless night I was dreading with the baby between the two of us.

Ten comes out of the bathroom and says, "I loved it when you made the old man blush... *'We're working on it'* was a cool answer. Come on, Lovey, get ready for bed. We've got work to do."

Chapter 21

Thank *God it's Friday!* I sing along as I hear the song playing on the radio when I walk by the electronics store a couple of blocks away from home. The music blasting from their speaker is so loud the baby jerked in me. Even though the sound must have been muffled by the amniotic fluid, it was enough to startle him... or her.

It's been a long winter and a trying one. I gave my resignation to Marc Martin in September, telling him that I was going to take a break and then open my own place. He wouldn't hear of it. He said I had to stay on and train someone else. The man's been so good to me there was no way I could refuse, so I stayed on until tonight.

My due date is February 15. I have four days to rest before pushing my third child into the world. Manhattan is packing up for a long weekend. The weather channel has announced a snowstorm. Yesterday I made sure we were stocked up for a few days without electricity. We have canned food, plenty of bottled water and candles. Tonight after I've taken my shower I'm filling up the bathtub.

During this pregnancy I've had a very hard time with smells, there's no way I'm going to be caught in a place where I can't flush.

I get home and free Catherine, our live-in girl. She's spending the weekend at her boyfriend's house in Brooklyn. She needs the rest, soon she's going to be helping me juggling two kids. She rushes out the second I get in. Alexandra's all cleaned and ready for bed. I throw my coat on the sofa and settle on the floor in her room to play with her giant Duplo farm. It's a present from Alexander. He has purchased every existing animal in addition to the box set so it's more like Noah's arc than a farm. I get a kick out of watching Alexandra using the lion and the tiger to shepherd the cattle back into her corale. Every so often, when I make animal sounds, there's a burst of laughter from both of us. Nothing's more delightful than a young child's giggles. She's such a cute little girl. She has a temper though. She can be adorable one instant and horrible the next. I smile thinking that it's probably what the people working with me have been thinking for the past weeks!

"Dada!" Alexandra screams and stretches her arm out. I look up and Ten is leaning on the door frame. He's got a few snowflakes in his hair and is all flushed from the cold. He picks her up and says, "Is my little princess ready for bed?"

She protests and he teases her. I roll over to a sitting position. I'm a regular blimp. As I try to stand up, I get a strange pain that makes me stop halfway in my movement. I freeze and take a deep breath. I'm not saying anything to Ten because if I do he'll freak out and we'll spend the weekend in the emergency room getting me monitored. I try moving again. I'm fine.

I manage to get back up and get our dinner started while Ten begins to read a bed time story to Alexandra. I know one can easily turn to a dozen if you let her. When our meal is ready I call the last story, give Alexandra a kiss and go lay down on the couch. I flip through the channels and the biggest news of the night is the snowstorm. The weatherman predicts that this February, 1983, snowstorm will be one we'll all remember. I look at the flurries through the window. It's lovely to watch the snow when you're warm and safe.

I close my eyes and when I open them again the lights are dimmed. I have a pillow under my head and a cover on my body. Ten's laying on the floor by my side reading a book.

"I'm sorry," I say. "I wanted to spend the evening with you. We've both been so busy. I've hardly seen you for weeks."

"Don't worry baby I'm not going anywhere for a few days," he point to the window and through the city lights I see that we're in the middle of some serious weather. I pull myself up and there's this weird pain again.

Ten is watching me and he notices this time.

"Are you all right?" he asks.

"Sure, I just forget that I'm so large I need to move more slowly," I say.

"You're not large," he says and I snort. He laughs, "Okay, you are but you're also magnificent. The last time he saw you, Jimmy said you looked like a splendid fertility goddess."

"Right, Laura and me, we're the two new fertility goddesses and we're going to populate the earth with little Clarks." I stop and realize I'm being silly. Who knows if Laura's baby is Jimmy or Steven's kid? Their life style sure is complicated. How do you work this out?

I pull myself up and walk to the corner window. The view is magnificent. Everything is pure white. There's no traffic in the street or in the avenue. A few pedestrians are walking by, probably rushing home. I realize that Oliver was supposed to be here tonight. I guess he got stuck at the hospital. He's only a dozen blocks away so he could walk back home. Probably some of the staff never showed because of the storm and he's stuck there.

The pain returns and I can hardly stand. I would feel so much safer if Oliver were here. I can't walk all those blocks to the hospital and I'm sure there are no ambulances available tonight.

"Ten," I want to ask him to call Oliver and find out if he's coming home.

"Yes dear," he answers without looking up. He's back in his book.

"Ten," I call out again. The room is spinning and I have a hard time breathing. I'm in a part of the room where there's nothing to hold on to. One more step and I'll be by the couch. Surely I can do one more step. I try and call out again, "Ten" before all starts turning to black. "Shit he's going to freak out," is the last thought I have as I fade away.

When I come around, Ten's face is over mine. He's trying to look cool but I know he's panicked.

"How do you feel?" he asks.

"Fine. I think," I go through a slow inventory of my sensations speaking out loud. "The back of my head is throbbing. Probably the result of my fall. The belly is a bit contracted but nothing painful. My legs are sticky."

"Yeah, your water broke," he says with a wary voice.

"What are you not telling me?" I ask. He knows this is a normal part of childbirth, he's seen it last time. Something else has to be bothering him.

"I don't remember it being so pink for Alexandra."

"Oh ... I'm surprised you were able to notice the color on the dark floor of the court house."

He ignores my comment and says, "I buzzed the doorman and asked if we had a midwife in the building. He consulted with the super and said we have a nurse who's been working in a hospice for the last twenty years, an eighty year old retired orthopedic surgeon, a shrink, and a recently graduated otolaryngologist."

I laugh at this inventory, "The recent graduate sounds like the best bet," I say.

"That's what I thought too but he's not home," Ten explains.

"We're going to be fine," I say. "Women had babies at home for centuries and..."

"The mortality rates were astounding," Ten says.

I try to joke. "You realize you're not being helpful?"

"Sorry baby, I'm so sorry." Ten hates being helpless.

"Did you call Oliver?"

"Of course. That's the first thing I did!"

"And?"

"He's finishing some surgery and coming over as quickly as he can."

"Good. He'll find a way to get here. We're going to be fine."

"You promise?" Ten's got tears in his eyes. "I don't know what I would do without you."

I pull him to me, "Stop it, silly. You're being dramatic for nothing! I'm not going anywhere."

I put his hand on my belly and say, "You see, no contractions. You're not allowed to panic before they're at full force and five minutes apart. In the meantime we're going to pick a name."

Ten wipes his eyes and tries to play along. "You remember you only get to pick the first name because he gets James as a middle name, right?"

"Yes, I was thinking about Oliver."

"What about Oliver?" Ten has never been so thick.

"Oliver, for the baby's name."

"Oh!" Now he gets it.

"If Oliver runs under the blizzard to come deliver this baby, I think we should call your son Oliver."

"Sure," he says. But at this point he's so worried that I could suggest something as exotic as Amadeus or Archibald he would have no objection.

"I'm going to close my eyes and rest now," I say. "I'm really tired."

I wake up again and all I see is the top of Oliver's head. He's got my legs bent and my knees spread out. He's got a hand into me. He's trying to ascertain the extent of the dilation.

"Hey, Doc," I say.

"Hey, Lyv." He looks at me and winks. "Thank you for bailing me out, otherwise I would have been stuck in the emergency room all night."

"Any time," I laugh. Only Oliver could consider my dragging him through the cold for twelve blocks as doing him a favor. "Where's Ten?"

"I sent him to kitchen and told him to boil water."

"What ever for?" I ask.

"To get him out of the way." Oliver's grinning. "That's what they always say in the cowboy movies when the woman is having a baby in the middle of nowhere."

I laugh again. Oliver has the strangest sense of humor.

"Tell me, Lyv, how do you feel?"

"Not bad but I'm concerned because I have no contractions. Since my water broke shouldn't the delivery process have started?" I ask.

"Not necessarily. If we were in the hospital I would just monitor you like we did for Alexandra but since we're at home I'm inducing you."

I notice there's an i.v. tube in my arm that is attached to a bottle hooked to one of our dining room chairs with some masking tape. Next to me there's this large first aid kit similar to the one the EMTs usually run out of the ambulances with. I'm sure it weighs a ton.

"Did you carry this for twelve blocks in the storm?" I ask.

"Nah" he says. "I have a friend who's a motocross nut, I called him up and he came to pick me up. He was so happy to have a reason to cross Manhattan at full speed tonight that he asked me to thank you for the opportunity."

I breathe deeply and say, "I think the contractions are starting."

"Good. It's the oxytocin I just gave you. It's normal."

I wait until the contractions subside and I ask, "Did you look at the amniotic fuid? Ten said it was bloody."

Oliver rolls his eyes and says, "He mopped it up with a navy blue towel so I can't tell." He shrugs when he adds, "but even if it was, pink is no big deal."

I feel a little better knowing pink can be okay. I'm exhausted. I think I like daytime deliveries better. I fall asleep between each contraction until Oliver asks me to stay awake. This is it. At the next one I'll have to push. Ten is kneeling behind me and supporting my back. He's got a wet towel and wipes my brow while whispering silly things in my ear. He says I'm so courageous he's in awe of me, that if I don't want to have other kids he'll be fine with it ...

"Oh please shut up!" I yell as I push forward for what I hope is the last time.

But he just can't stop, "I'm sorry baby, I didn't mean to upset you."

Not a second too soon, the baby's out and I laugh as I hear a wail. "It's a boy," Oliver says as he clamps the cord and then wraps the baby in a clean towel.

"Welcome home Oliver," I say.

Both Olivers are looking at me. There's my little baby who's a few seconds old and seems to be taking in the world very seriously and then there's my sweet doctor who's taken a few seconds to register that the baby was going to be named after him.

"Oh, right. Oliver. Cool choice," Oliver is hiding his emotion behind his professional facade but I can see he's happy.

Ten is teary eyed again and kissing my forehead. "I love you, Lyv," he says.

"I love you too," I answer.

Oliver puts my baby boy in my arms with the cord still attached and he's the most handsome baby ever. I think he looks like his dad. I realize I'm probably delirious but it's a good thing since I'm deliriously happy.

Life is so full of surprises, I never would have thought this would be what my happy ever after would look like.

To be continued.

ABOUT THE AUTHOR

Born in Manhattan, Olivia Rigal spent her youth going back and forth between the United States and France.

She lived and studied law in both countries.

While studying she kept herself busy with a variety of jobs.

She worked in the Clignancourt Flea Market as well as in a Parisian recording studio.

In Manhattan, she was a dog groomer and then an administrative assistant in a famous English auction house.

Olivia settled in France to raise her family.

She travelled throughout South East Asia and has a special fondness for Laos and Thailand.

When her law practice does not keep her busy in Paris, she runs away to write novels in her Florida home next to MacArthur Beach State Park.

In December 2012 she started publishing short novels in English as an independent. Early 2014, she began translating them into French.

Most stories she tells stand alone. However her characters often meet so you can run into them again in several stories.

She loves to chat with readers so feel free to drop her a line at *me@oliviarigal.com* or visit her Facebook page

www.facebook.com/AuthorOliviaRigal

Other books by Olivia RIGAL

IRON TORNADOES MC ROMANCE

- **Stone Cold.** Lisa Mayfield returns home from law school to a dead brother and a former lover she no longer recognizes. Brian Hatcher, her brother's best friend, dropped out of the police academy. Instead of working with Lisa's brother to bring down organized crime, he became a full-patched member of the Iron Tornadoes, an outlaw motorcycle club, the very one that may have caused her brother's fall. Searching for answers to how her David died, Lisa can't ignore the attraction she still feels for Brian. The chemistry is undeniable but is there anything left of the boy she once loved or has he turned into a stone cold biker?

- **Cold Burn**. Brian Hatcher wants it all - control of the motorcycle club his father runs, the murderer of his best friend David six feet under, and, more than anything, David's sister Lisa. He wants Lisa on the back of his bike, in his home, in his bed, and under the spell of his cold burn. But, with Lisa unsure of the role the Iron Tornadoes played in her brother's death and her long-held goal of becoming a criminal prosecutor, what Brian wants may be nothing like what Brian gets.

- **Cold Fusion**. When he graduates from the Police Academy, David Mayfield is no rookie. His past experience as an MP allows him to jump right into an undercover mission. Hired at the Bush Fire, a strip club owned by the white supremacist group David's task force is investigating, he is to gather information.

But fascinated by Jeanne-Michelle, a curvaceous Haitian dancer, he soon realizes that the real challenge of his mission may turn out to be abiding by the single rule of the strip club: "No messing around with the talent."

- **Hot Pursuit.** *In progress.*

AS THEY PLEASE

- **As he bids.** Applying for a summer internship at an upscale auction house just because she has a mad crush on one of the bosses, may be Career Fail 101 for Hannah Cohen. Certainly, she is heading that way when she spends her first week focusing more on the way Bruce Nelson's mouth shapes his words than their actual meaning.

- **As She Begs.** After Hannah's second week under the close supervision of Bruce Nelson takes an unexpected twist, her first reaction is to run. And when Bruce vanishes instead of demanding an explanation, Hannah learns the hard way that in his world she will only get as good As She Begs.

LYV'S FAMILY

- **Jaded.** For a 22-year-old girl genius, few things are a challenge. Just don't introduce Jade Cooper to a bowl of ice cream or ask her to have a normal conversation, especially if you're a guy. Assisting her childhood friend on a research project in Southeast Asia, Jade doesn't expect her generous curves or men to be a problem. But even the best-laid plans of the exceptionally smart can go awry. Enter Oliver Wild, a charming stone expert who thinks normal is overrated and curves - not to mention Jade's world - are meant to be rocked.

- **Eve Trilogy.**

Naughty CHRISTMAS EVE - Eve is a curvaceous American living in Paris. She falls under the spell of a fellow lawyer on her way to Florida and finds out how hot a Christmas Eve can get in Miami ...

Sexy NEW YEAR'S EVE - but when she wakes up to an empty bed and moves on to Palm Beach to visit her family, the open arms of her ex fiancé look pretty comforting.

Spicy VALENTINE'S EVE - Back in Paris, Eve knows she is not cut out to have a man in every port. So the time has come, she needs to make a choice ... unless of course by the time she makes her mind up there's no choice left to make.

LEARNING CURVES

- Learning Curves 1: French Cooking 101

- Learning Curves 2: Advanced French Kissing

- Learning Curves 3: Detention

- Learning Curves 4: Graduation.

The voluptuous "Ariane," owner of a cooking school in France, has has organized an intensive weekend workshop that brings together a like-able cast of characters including an author, a newlywed couple, a cute actor, and a middle aged woman and her younger brother. A sexy relationship begins between Ariane and Peter, the "student" with whom she shared an attraction from book one. But Peter goes home to America, promising to return. Meanwhile, Ariane, continues her life (under the gentle bit watchful eye of her elderly, wealthy landlady, Madame Caroline).

Peter does come back to Paris, but Ariane finds that sometimes the reality is not as delicious as the fantasy. What is so lovely about the Learning Curves series as I see it, is that Ariane might live in Paris, but she's "every woman, everywhere" in many ways. She is on a journey of discovery and we, the readers, get to follow it. In most women's lives, the path of love, romance, career, friends, and so forth isn't always a perfectly smooth path. Every decision Ariane has to make, every obstacle thrown in her way, every choice, will change her life. And isn't that what makes life and romance, so exciting?

Olivia Rigal makes the dialogue and the plot lines realistic and fun to follow, and the romance elements are just steamy enough to keep your interest without the author resorting to graphic sex. Masterfully done.

Alison Blackman Dunham – www.advicesisters.com